FEELING LIKE A BEACHED WHALE

Tammy Page

ISBN: 978-1-5272-8311-4

First published 2021

A light-hearted fiction about a young woman named Sophie whose body clock is ticking so she decides it's time for her and her hubby to have a baby. Share with her the journey of pregnancy and the funny bits that are rarely told or spoken about when deciding to have a baby.

Good morning, good afternoon or good evening.

To whenever you have decided to pick up my book, I would firstly like to say thank you for buying my first attempt at writing, it's a very nervous moment for me but I really do appreciate it.

Secondly, I'd also like to explain a few issues within the book before you read it.

I decided 10 years ago that I'd like to write a book. Now, I'm no writer, I hated English at school and I thought 'What a waste of time this is' … how wrong was I! I struggled with learning, I am very much a practical person rather than an academic.

So as you read through my book, you ***will*** find grammatical mistakes! I don't apologise for them, they are part of me and this book and not everything in life is perfect.

So, I guess what I am trying to say is, no matter what your background or education, if you want to do something, DO IT! Don't let anything or anyone hold you back…enjoy!

Contents

PROLOGUE

Sophie

Hi . . . I've just started the biggest adventure of my life by having a BABY.

My name is Sophie, nice to meet you.

It all started last year when all my friends decided to start having babies.

I was quite happy with my life until that point; I loved my job, I was happily married and we had a baby . . . our dog. I think with all this chat of friends having babies it started my body clock ticking which is weird seeing I didn't think I had one.

It was always in the evening when I was watching some boring telly that I started to think: I'd quite like a baby, most of my friends have done it and some of them are right wimps so it can't be that bad. Plus I would like our children to be close in age so they can be friends . . . wouldn't want it to start off a loner, life being cruel enough at times - let's try and give it some friends to start off with.

So, after a few months of going back and forth over the idea we thought we would go for it, that's when it all began.

CHAPTER ONE

ME

Everywhere I look I see pregnant women, every magazine has an interview with the latest pregnant celebrity, they all look so beautiful, flawless skin, glowing, great hair, basically just a whole package of beauty - well all I can say is, airbrushing has a lot to answer for!

MONDAY 22nd OCTOBER 2018

As I previously said, my husband Liam and I are thinking of starting a family, so I decided to make an appointment with the family planning clinic. The clinic is an old church hall, in the corner of the hall is a women sitting behind an old school desk writing down patients names and telling them to go and sit down to fill out a form. Looking around the hall I could see other people filling out forms. The majority of the patients looked to be about 15 years old, no parents with them, just their mates, with a mixture of girls and boys I felt as If I was in a youth club. I watched as a boy came out of a make-shift, curtained room nodding to his mate which I assumed was to tell him to get up and stop reading the leaflets. The lad looked embarrassed as they put their heads down and scuttled off out of the building. I wonder why he was there but obviously I'm not going to find out as that's something you can't really ask a doctor, why their last patient was here but I felt he looked shifty.

However, speaking with a lovely doctor who advised me not to worry if it takes a while as I had been on the pill for a good number of years and it might take a while to fall pregnant.

My very dear friend Louise already had a baby and is now pregnant with her second and she wants two more after this one comes out. Personally I think she's got a screw loose but I can actually see her raising the Brady Bunch. The conversation came up about birthing partners and somehow, I've ended up being hers! I did say how I didn't think it was a great idea as I faint on smear tests but her answer was, 'You'll be fine, it will be kill or cure for you.'

You see, I have an irrational fear ever since I was young that I would die giving birth and I really like living so I would rather not DIE.

Louise says it's nothing like what you see on the telly, there is really no need for all that screaming but I just think she is abnormally strong, like the Hulk. The rest of us need to have a little scream every now and then but we shall soon find out I'm sure.

In my job as a hairdresser I get to talk to a lot of people and everyone who has had children seems to delight you with the extended version of their own experience of childbirth and nearly every single one sounds horrific.

They all end the story with, "Don't worry Soph, you forget the pain and it's the most natural thing in the world." Hey, have you lot all been smoking crack???? Something that big coming out of something that small does not sound natural to me. Still, when I took a few moments to process it I realised I see many more younger women having babies and I mean they do seem to be getting younger and younger. If that church hall was anything to go by so it can't be that bad . . . can it?

The clinic said a year so I thought we had plenty of time to prepare ourselves and somehow get over my irrational fear of dying.

CHAPTER TWO

THE PARTNER

THURSDAY 25th OCTOBER 2018

So I got the call.

There I was in the middle of my sign language class which I am absolute rubbish at by the way because the only thing I can sign is 'bullshit' and 'my name is'. I suppose I could put it all together: 'My name is bullshit' and I have a sentence. Anyway, I left the class signing what I believed was me having to go but really it was me just waving my arms around in the air a lot. I got in my car and rang my hubby to tell him I was needed but also to tell him I was shitting it and why did I agree to this? He wished me luck and told me to pull myself together knowing how much of a total wimp I am.

Once I had to put a plaster on his finger and I passed out on our living room floor for ten minutes. You can see how he thinks me being a birthing partner is a really bad idea but as a good husband, he's supporting my decision . . . what a fool!

So I speed off at 5mph, the speed limit in the school and arrive at the hospital to find Louise clinging to the door of her auntie's car whilst Auntie was off trying to find a wheelchair. My first words that escaped my mouth were, "Are you ok?" followed by the thought that of course she's not bloody ok, she's going to be pushing a grapefruit out of something the size of a pea.

Looking at my friend panting at the car door I knew it really wasn't a good idea me being there so if I slowly walked away she would never know. However, just at that moment the wheelchair arrived and I found myself steering it through to the labour ward thinking nothing but bloody hospital wheelchairs that only seem to work if you drag them backwards. Poor Louise, in between her contractions she had to deal with me bashing her into every wall possible on the way to the labour suite.

I remember it well: I follow a midwife to a small room, I'm not sure even if she knew we were behind her but I decided I was going to follow her anyway as she clearly had a sense of direction and knew where she was going. Louise's husband Daniel helps Louise out of the wheelchair and onto the bed and I can't help notice that everyone in this room seems quite relaxed especially Daniel; he's taking it all in in his stride. It's just me having a mild panic attack! In my head of course, on the outside I look as cool as a cucumber (yeah right).

The midwives appear. One's a student and the other looks like a Great Britain champion in women's shotput. Louise is asked if she minds the student being there and her reply, that it's fine, amazes me. Wow, she's so relaxed and I'm starting to calm down. Louise is doing remarkably well and doesn't look like she's in too much pain. She's not having any pain relief yet so I'm starting to think Louise was right: it's not that bad. An hour has passed, and things really start to KICK OFF! Louise looks like she's in agonising pain and the contractions are closer together with the midwives appearing a lot more. Suddenly the gas and air is wheeled through the door and finally I'm asked, "Can you fit two masks to that please?" It seems I've been put in charge of gas and air, water and wet towels while Daniel appears to be in a state of shock, standing by Louise's side . . . holding her hand . . . staring at her without blinking. He's been like this for a while now.

My panic had started to return; it's a horrible thing to see someone in so much pain and know there is nothing you can do about it. Louise has the gas and air clenched between her teeth. The midwives are still having a casual chat, stopping every now and then to tell her how well she is doing. How bloody patronizing -of course she's doing well, she's pushing a human out of her foofoo!

This stage of labour seems to last forever and I can see Louise is starting to get tired, muttering, "I can't do it anymore, just leave it in there." Top dog midwife suggests trying to speed things up a bit by breaking her waters. OH GOD WHAT DOES THAT EVEN MEAN? I'm starting to have another panic attack; how many is that so far?

Top dog asks if the student can be included which of course in my head I'm shouting, NO NO NO but Louise nods her head in exhaustion, "Yeah, that's fine" whilst biting down onto the gas and air. I stumble aimlessly around the room trying to remember the simple act of breathing just as Top dog and student walk back through the door with what looks like a giant knitting needle . . . Oh hold on, it IS a giant knitting needle!

I'm surprised that I am not checking for holes in my eyelids on the floor at this point knowing where they're going to shove the aforementioned massive needle but somehow, I have managed to keep it together. I look away as I didn't want to have the image of where they are putting it burn through my retinas but top dog midwife is still within earshot. "Now, have you done it right?" I'm thinking, well I bloody hope so, oh and can you just hurry up as I can't control this not fainting malarkey forever?

Louise is still very much in pain but is in total control, not even whingeing or moaning. I know I certainly would be if I had a huge knitting needle shoved in me. Suddenly there is a gush of water. Jesus, how much water is in there? It's like Niagara Falls. When Louise pipes up with a groan and how lovely and warm it is, I've already decided that if this is what gas and air does for you, I'm definitely having some! We manage to keep the water contained on the bed with what looks like giant puppy training mats but as I try to pull them away from under her, Louise growls at me so I'm smart enough to leave them be.

The sounds from the other rooms are very concerning. I can hear a lot of screaming; what are they doing to those poor women? Oh god is this what we have to come? Wait, have we not had the bad part yet?

Louise suddenly turns into the incredible hulk and grabs my hand, oh my days, the pain... I wanted to complain or even just let out a little whimper but I thought better of it. Luckily, I'm a hairdresser so it's not like I need my hands at all!

My fingers have started to swell and go purple. I'm wondering if your fingers can drop off if the circulation is cut off for too long when the midwife pipes up with a shout: HERE COMES THE BABY! Top dog says the baby is about to crown and it might sting a little . . . STING?? I can think of a more honest word than sting! At last I began to get really excited and I heard myself encouraging her. "You can do this, just keep breathing, you're doing so well!" like I was like a fan at a football match cheering on the favourite player.

All at once, the head was out, and Top Dog suggests she takes a breather for a moment: "You've only got the shoulders to get out, once those are out, it's easy."

I mean, really? The small human should have a torso, legs and arms, I'm not sure it's going to be that easy. But sure enough, once those shoulders are out the baby is basically dragged out.

IT'S A BOY!!!!

The baby has been born, it was amazing! I just kept looking at him and looking at Louise, thinking: How the hell did all that fit in there when he's massive and where do your organs go whilst he's in there and what happens now, do your organs just float back down to their original home????

In my state of shock, I hadn't realized that the cord hadn't yet been cut when Student Midwife asks Daniel if he wants to do it. I look over to him, he is still staring at Louise and I don't think he has blinked yet but he declines the offer of cord cutting. That's when Top Dog looks over to me nodding her head towards me and then the cord. My first reaction is HELL NO but then I take a huge intake of labour room air and think about when I'd ever get this opportunity again and if I faint now, at least the baby is out. So I take the scissors from Top Dog and proceed to cut away; who knew it was so tough? Jesus, it was like cutting squishy rope – yuck!

It's amazing you know, just five minutes ago Louise was in excruciating pain and now she looks so relaxed and so in love with her beautiful baby that maybe she was right; this was kill or cure and I think it has cured me.

I step to other side of the room, relieved that everyone is ok. Louise is fine, the baby is fine and I think Daniel is fine as he has at least blinked again which I think is a good sign. Top dog says, "Well done Louise, just one more bit to deliver the placenta" and with that, my mind is blown! Wait, what do they mean it's not over? I thought that just got dragged that out with the baby . . . apparently not!

Top dog returns to the room saying that the baby has been in this world half an hour now and still no sign of the placenta so she suggests something to help speed things along. Unfortunately, that would bring her contractions back. I look at Louise in dread and say to her quietly . . ."I can get rid of her if you want me to?" I tell her to leave it in there but apparently you can't, so it looks like the end is not yet.

Louise has been given the dreaded injection to bring the contractions back and I can see her face scrunch up. She looks like a bull dog chewing on a wasp and that's how I know it's beginning to work but a few contractions later and the placenta is out. OH MY DAYS IT'S MASSIVE! Now I'm definitely perplexed as to how it all fitted in there, how has she even been walking around with all that weight? Speaking of weight, the student midwife whipped the placenta away to weigh it and check it? Why? Surely it's junk now, why the check and weigh? I'm assuming Top Dog saw my confused expression and explains that they check to see if it's all there. She was actually holding it up like a piece of meat exclaiming that if you hold it up towards the light on a sunny day it can actually look like a stain glass window . . .WHAT THE ACTUAL F**K! I can't believe I've let this women look after Louise, she clearly has problems if she thinks a placenta can look like a stain glass window!

Now absolutely everything has been delivered – yes, I did ask just to make sure - I'm not sure I could watch anything else come out of Louise's body. At one point, it was like watching a magician keep pulling the handkerchiefs out of the sleeves but instead of silk it was a small human and mess.

Top Dog returns again, she's like Batman, but this time she has an industrial sized torch. What does she need that for? Maybe she's expecting a power cut. Top Dog sets the torch down on the bed next to Louise's legs and in a low calm voice says, "I just need to do a little bit of repair work down there." Repair work? Oh Christ, tonight has been a real eye opener and so many questions . . . repair work?

As I'm questioning this, Top Dog drags in the gas and air again which tells me this isn't going to be pleasant. She tells Louise to pop her feet into what I can only describe as huge stirrups . . . Oh wait, these really are huge stirrups - she's not going bloody horse riding!

I stand the other side of the room trying to take deep breaths and to keep my eyes on the beautiful new baby boy but I just can't help feeling faint again. Do you know how draining it is being such a wimp? Top Dog notices my corpse-like complexion and tells me to sit down before I fall down seeing as she 'hasn't got time to pick me up off the floor as she has stitch work to do.' The woman has such a way with words.

I take a seat next to Louise who has already clamped down onto the gas and air whilst Top Dog has now positioned herself on a stool at the bottom of the bed directly between Louise's legs. The huge torch has also been placed there and from this end it looks like the sun is being reborn through Louise's legs. Top dog has her concentration face on which I'm glad about because that's the last place you want mucked up and I'm assuming it's pretty mucked up now without her important stitch work.

Repair work done, the legs are out of the horse harness and Louise is now enjoying a cup of tea and a KitKat. Daniel is reading a paper which is good because earlier I thought his eyes were going to be stuck in one position forever; even if he just looks at the pictures in the paper at least his eyes are having a little work out. The new baby boy is sleeping soundly in his temporary crib. It's time for me to leave this gorgeous new little family in peace, I say my goodbyes and tell Louise how in awe I am of her and that she's my all-time hero!

I get in my car at 1.50am and head home still in shock at what I've just witnessed, part of me amazed and the other part of me horrified. Maybe I should put the brakes on having a baby for a while.

CHAPTER THREE

THE TALK

FRIDAY 26th OCTOBER 2018

Fridays are always busy days at work, no time to think, eat or even pee.

I walk into the salon and my mum asks how Louise is.

Oh God yeah! I saw a human being born last night and the images keep flashing back to me, breathe Sophie, just breathe.

Just to let you know I work with my mother (or as I like to call her, Smother as she worries about anything and everything (LOVE HER). Smother or her real name Jackie has always been a hairdresser and at the tender age of six I knew I wanted to follow in my mum's footsteps into the crazy world of hair. As a child I loved spending time in the salon watching my mum work her magic. The salon was always warm vibrant and full of laughs, proper laughs like deep down in your belly laughs. Her energy for life and hair has always been infectious and just about everyone that came into contact with her felt special and went out looking bloody fabulous, so how could I not want join in on all the Crazyness.......

For some reason though people think not only are we hairdressers but we should also be magicians. Little tip for you all: if your hair has been dyed Jet black you are NOT going to be a beautiful platinum blonde like the picture of Gwen Stefani you have so kindly brought in to show me. Expect to be a ginger ninja first, so if on the other hand you've brought me in a picture of Ginger Spice then perfect, my job will be done. Bleaching takes time and skill the slower the lift the better the blonde….. remember that ladies.

Salon life is amazing but tough so if you think hair is an option when deciding your life path then think again.

Here's a little insight into the world of hair:

1. You must always wear a smile on your face even if inside you're really wanting to tell everyone to shut the f**k up and go do one.
2. Not only are you a hairdresser, you are also a counsellor to all your clients' troubles and woes.
3. You need to perfect the art of getting into someone's head so that when your client says she wants a change you need to decode whether she actually means it or if she means just half a shade lighter / darker that to anyone else's eyes no one will notice but God forgive you if you do actually give her a real change for she will endeavour to make you feel like the shittiest hairdresser ever to have lived.
4. Train your bladder. Many times have I got to 4 o'clock and had the first pee of the day. I know it's not good for you but when you have one colour developing whilst blow-drying someone else as you see your next lady being shampooed, thinking of going to the toilet seems to go out the window.
5. Clients that show up late and think its okay: I get it if the traffic is bad or road works you didn't know about but just pressing your snooze button three times to give yourself an extra 20 mins in bed, NO, NO, NO. We hairdressers work by strict timings so if

your first lady is late it's going to put you out for the rest of the day. Professionalism means you mustn't show you're slightly annoyed, you must smile and tell your lovely client that it's fine, no need to worry even if inside your head you're counting slowly to ten!

6. Clients that turn their head to talk to you whilst cutting their hair even though you've told them numerous times to keep their head still and keep it in the position that you've put it in; how am I supposed to get a perfect precision cut when they are swinging their heads back and forth like Willow Smith. It's annoyingly frustrating, just so you know.

So if you can deal with all of that then roll up and come and play.

Finishing work feels good today as I am soooo tired. I pull up onto the drive and Liam is already home as I walk through the door, Chinese in one hand, wine in the other. I just cannot wait to stuff my face and chill out. Liam looks at me.

"So how was it?"

"How was what?"

"The birth"

"Oh f**k yeah it was horrendous, did you know the placenta when held up towards the light looks like a stain glass window?"

"WHAT?

"I know, gross. Hey, so listen Liam, I've been thinking, we are good the way we are, right?"

"Oh Soph, I knew it was a bad idea you being a birthing partner but what you want is to wait, right?"

"Yeah I know it is silly, it's probably just scared me a bit, are you sure you don't mind?"

"No it's fine, we could probably do with one more holiday anyway. I'll tell you what, I'll start looking now."

Wow, that was easy, I thought that chat was going to take a lot longer - thank god he wants another holiday first!

I sit down with my Chinese and oh my, it was delicious. Now for the wine and guilty pleasure trash TV.

"So Soph, you know you said you wanted to wait to have baby, are you sure? I know you are probably in shock right now but I'm just about to press Go on a holiday to a little Greek island and I don't need to hear in a week that you have changed your mind."

"No Liam, I'm sure. I've just watched many things come out of Louise's body that my mind is still trying to process and I think it may take a while, so go right ahead and book it up, baby."

CHAPTER FOUR

HALLOWEEN PARTY

SAT 27TH OCTOBER 2018

It's been a week since Louise brought life into this world and everything is good.

It's the weekend and getting very close to Halloween and Liam and I thought it would be a good idea to throw a Halloween party and tonight's the night. Preparation is underway and we've got cobwebs hanging over the oven; nothing new there, I do cook, I'm just not that great at it. Poor Liam does try and look enthusiastic when I do cook but I know secretly most of the time he's just waiting until I leave the room to give it to our dog. Anyway, sorry I've gone off point. Okay, so decorations are up, the booze has been bought and we have even spent out on a new firepit to toast marshmallows ....I looooooooovvvveee marshmallows.

It's 6pm and I'm upstairs transforming myself into something scary but I am not getting very far as I keep running out of wine . . . should have just brought the bottle upstairs. The party is supposed to kick off at 7 but no-one ever turns up on time, do they?

8pm and most people are here, I'm very impressed at the effort most people have made apart from a few who think drawing a few whiskers on their cheeks is good enough. No, no, no but I'll forgive them seeing as I've had a couple of wines.

FEELING LIKE A BEACHED WHALE

Drinks are flowing well, Liam and his mate Paul are well tanked up as they are the only ones dancing in the garden next to the firepit, slow dancing that is with hands perfectly placed: one hand on a butt cheek, the other in the small of each other's back. If I didn't know these two well, I would be slightly concerned by the nature of their relationship. All the face paint on our friends' faces have started to melt, all beginning to look like dodgy cartoon characters. It's 1am, I'm knackered, most people have gone and to the people that are still here I think I have made it clear I've had enough as I have taken myself upstairs to put my dressing gown on. Paul is the last one left . . . surprise surprise. I've decided to leave them to it and go to bed although it's a funny sight to see CHUCKY and KILLER CLOWN in my front room playing cards and drunkenly saying they love one another.

SUNDAY 28TH OCTOBER 2018

Woken up feeling like death; my mouth is like a cat's litter tray, my head feels like it has been put in a vice and my body feels like a 90 year-old.

I slowly lift my broken body to the edge of the bed where I steady myself to sit up straight . . . oh God, I think I'm gonna vom! I lay back down and curse myself for being such a knob head, I didn't think I drank that much last night but I'm a total lightweight, it's really no surprise why I feel like death is upon me.

1 hour later . . .

I finally make it downstairs. I feel like I deserve a trophy for making it this far down to another level as the journey downstairs feels like the return journey from Everest. I almost wanted to phone a friend to tell them I have arrived down to the hallway safely.

Standing in the hallway looking at the carnage that awaits me in the kitchen, I find myself pondering whether I can face it just at this moment in time. I walk into the living room to find my husband asleep on the sofa, his Ginger hair/ hat has fallen off so that the top of his forehead is bright white but from temple down is a weird mixture of colours that I cannot even describe, and the stench of the room is enough to make any human vomit. It smells somewhere in-between a gone off kebab and a rotting carcass.

I back up slowly out of the room fearful of 1:I was going to vomit from the smell and 2: the half Chucky would wake up and I can't deal with another hungover human right now. This is my moment, it's all about me and I don't need the competition of who feels worse. I lean myself against the door frame and slowly turn my head towards the direction of the kitchen knowing that it's not going to clean itself. It's moments like this I wish I was Harry Potter to just be able to cast a spell to clean itself; I do lift my arm and wave it up and down whilst chanting, 'Clean, Clean, Clean' but guess what? Nothing happens: BOLLOCKS!

I manage to lift my body off the door frame and inhale a deep intake of stagnant stale air and head towards the kitchen. It is worse than I first thought: empty beer cans in the washing machine, the floor, a ton of fake blood spilled across it and there is what looks like vomit in the sink. GROSS. I open the back door to air the room only to find our cat sitting on the step with a headless pigeon (oh yeah I forgot to say we also have a psycho cat). W.T.A.F. Why, why, why would you do this to me today of all days? Is this my punishment because I tried to make you wear a cat cape? He just sits there licking his paw, looking up at me with his evil psycho eyes and saunters off leaving me standing helpless above a decapitated pigeon.

ENOUGH IS ENOUGH - time to wake the beast!

I burst into the room yelling, "IT'S TIME TO GET UP! Psycho has bought us a headless . . . hold that thought, it's no good, I'm gonna vom."

I run upstairs . . . why didn't we buy a house with a downstairs loo? I hate being sick, I just want my mum who would make it all better although I think on this occasion, she would just slap me for drinking too much.

Liam keeps calling me asking me questions as if I can answer him whilst projectile vomit is flying out of my mouth (KNOBHEAD).

Why am I so ill when I really didn't drink much last night?

When I've finished bringing up the lining of my stomach I bum my way down the stairs figuring that the standing position isn't doing it for me and again I reach the hallway. Déjà vu.

I peer through the living room door to see Liam half sitting up scowling and muttering at me. I'm guessing it's not the words of you look so beautiful in the mornings darling. Nope, he's actually asking why the hell I've woken him and, "Jesus babe, you look rough."

So with my confidence through the roof I carry on trying to tell him he needs to drag his sorry arse carcass off the sofa to deal with the decapitated pigeon. He slowly gets up staring at me as he passes with angry eyes; I'm not sure why this is my fault but to be honest I couldn't give a rat's arse, I feel too ill to care.

3 HOURS LATER:

The kitchen is sparkling again, I think I'm high from bleach fumes. Liam has dealt with the pigeon and cleaned the living room as my nose just couldn't deal with that stench anymore.

I'm happy again with the house back to its beautiful self. I feel my mind can slow down again as I just can NOT cope with an untidy house, it's now time to chill and eat my body weight in comfort food!

CHAPTER FIVE

FINDING OUT

MONDAY 29TH OCTOBER 2018

I wake up loving the fact I don't have to get up. That's one good thing about hairdressers: most salons shut on Mondays. Happy days for me but not for Liam who gets up feeling jealous of me still snuggled up still in bed. I can't help but gloat in my position, making a little murmur to rub in the fact it's so warm and cosy - I know I'm a bitch but I don't care at this moment in time. Liam is rushing around making a huge amount of noise for this unearthly time in the morning then just like that, silence strikes the house; he's finally gone to work. Liam works for a telephone company fixing phone lines and other stuff, I should really listen more to what he actually does. Note to self, listen to the husband more about his work!

I take a moment to appreciate the silence and the feeling of comfort I feel in a warm snug bed when suddenly that sick feeling returns, coming over all hot and sweaty. Surely this can't be a two-day hangover? It must be a bug. I sit up in the bed thinking maybe I'm just too cosy and it's just that my body needs a bit of air but sadly no. So I decide to get up, making me angry as I had visions of staying in bed until at least 10am. I head downstairs to see if a cup of tea will make me feel better (you can never go wrong with a cuppa) but today even just the smell of the tea is putting me off.

Let's try some breakfast, something light like Shreddies. Billy our dog is looking up at me as if to say, are you going to feed me at all today? So I lean into his doggy bin to get his food out and WHAM BAM just like that, the smell has made me vomit into his dog bowl. Billy is still sitting there patiently waiting, cocking his head looking at me. Oh my days, I feel rough - at least it was contained into a bowl though, high five to me! I wash the dog bowl and take myself back upstairs as I think I am safer up there near a loo. I text Liam to see how he's feeling and he calls me to tell me he is as fit as a fiddle. Why he couldn't just text me that I don't know, most probably to rub my face in it as I was gloating earlier. I bet he is loving the fact I'm sick, well he's the one that will be cooking later, not me because I'm too poorly. He will not be liking that, ha, gutted!

It is now 9pm and I'm feeling much better so I decide to eat which to everyone's delight, stays down, whoop, whoop! I still decide to get an early night as its back into the crazy world of hair tomorrow, nighty night.

TUESDAY 30TH OCTOBER 2018

Woken up by the sound of psycho cat coughing up a hair ball. God I bet you're jealous of my life. Looking at him doing that haunch head bobbing thing that cats do when trying to get something up, I can't help thinking that he does this on purpose even though he clearly isn't. He is a bit of a knobbish cat like that, I think he hates me. He's more Liam's cat than mine and I suspect he is secretly trying to plot a plan to kill me. Anyway enough of Psycho he's taken up too much of this page already, so I suppose now I am awake I'd better get up to make myself world-ready. I make myself tea and again I'm hating it but forcing it down - I cannot stand coffee and let me tell you no no-one wants to deal with me not having my tea.

It's 8.20 and I'm now leaving for work. I like to get in early to get my mind ready for the day ahead. Driving along singing away to Whitney and yes I sound just like her . . . in a parallel universe. But I don't care, I'm giving it a go - thank God my windows are up though. Don't you think it's funny when you see someone else driving along singing? Do you ever play the game Guess that Song? I know you never find out what song they are actually singing but that just means you win every time so happy days all round.

Today is a busy day in the salon which I'm happy about as when you feel poorly, sometimes the best thing to do is to keep busy. Let's just hope I don't vomit on anyone's head. Again, weird thing about hairdressing: when you're ill, some clients don't seem to understand this, given the majority do but some think life is just so unfair seeing they've booked and it's typical that I'm ill. What can I say? I end up apologising for being sick, I know I shouldn't but when you care about your work so much you feel guilty even if you are sitting out the back with your head between your legs.

Nearly home time. All that is left to do is cash up, fold the towels for the next day and tell all the girls they can go. Time for me to go home but before I do, I think I'll just pop into Asda for some comfort food like soup. Why is it when you're poorly, it's always soup to the rescue? Because it's magic! Walking round Asda carrying a basket, I act like I'm on Supermarket Sweep then suddenly supermarket sweep has become a World's Strongest Man event with the full basket that I'm struggling to carry. I pass down the sickness aisle, the one with all the meds and my eye catches a pregnancy test box . . . SHIT! No, I can't be. Or maybe I bloody can be. Oh dear, maybe this is why I feel like poo?

Don't panic Soph, just balance it on top of everything else and buy it, I am trying to talk myself calm. It's probably a bug anyway.. but the tea? When you feel like shit who wants tea? And the smells? Dog food and Liam stink all the time anyway so maybe that's not a valid argument. Feeling sick? Ok it's all stacking up but I'm your calm side, don't drag me over to the dark side, just pull yourself together, pay for the abundance of cheese you have brought then get your arse home and wee on a stick. Then we will know for sure, okay? Good, glad I cleared that up.

I arrive home and oh good, Liam is still at work, what a result as I am not sure I can hide my sheer panic from him. Get in wee on the stick job done, get inside panic about weeing on the stick, walk around like a headless chicken for a bit, sweat some more then wee on the stick. Wow, 5 minutes is a long time when you're not sure what you want the stick to say. Well, obviously it can't talk but you know what I mean.

I hear the door bang downstairs. Shit, Liam is home! I poke my head out of the bathroom door and yell that I'll be down in a min but he doesn't even respond, he just makes his way up the stairs to get changed then tries to talk to me through the bathroom door.

"How was your day?"

"Feeling a bit weird to be honest, hoping it's just a bug."

"What do you mean hoping it just a bug, what else can it be?"

"Give me one minute and I'll tell you."

Sitting on the loo looking at the little stick, I keep reading it then re-reading it: OH BLOODY HELL! "LIAM!"

Liam comes rushing to the bathroom. "Are you ok Soph?"

"'IM PREGNANT!"

"WHAT?"

"I'M PREGNANT!"

"Oh ok, are you sure?"

"Pretty sure. Here, you read it"

"Well, what am I looking at?"

"The lines, Liam, the lines."

"Soph, you're going to need to explain this a little more. What do the lines mean?"

"That I am BLOODY PREGNANT, YOU DOUGNUT! WHAT DO THINK THEY MEAN?"

"Ok Soph, don't get too worked up about this, it's ok."

"What do you mean it's ok? A week ago I watched Louise's fanny be stretched to the size of a watermelon!"

Liam is now laughing. I don't think any of this is remotely funny, I feel like shit and still have the images of Louise's birth lasered onto my brain.

"Soph listen, you are an amazing women, you are funny, caring, beautiful, strong, kind . . . I couldn't think of anyone better to become the mother of my child than you. Think how cute it's going to be and with a mummy like you, it's already the luckiest little thing."

I'm crying like a baby now, jeez how much water is coming out of my eyes?

"Liam, are you sure you want this? We just booked a holiday!"

"Oh yeah, you're right. No, it's not the best time, let's make an appointment for tomorrow to get rid of it . . . you can be stupid sometimes Soph, of course I want it. I'm so happy I am going to be a DADDY. Are you sure though Soph? Even though I'm happy, this is your body at the end of the day, I'll support you with whatever you decide."

"Well Yes, I think I'm ok, I am just shocked at the moment. It needs to sink in but I think it's going to be okay, isn't it?"

CHAPTER SIX

THE EARLY DAYS

WEDNESDAY 31st OCTOBER 2018

It's a funny thing finding out you're pregnant because your life changes in an instant; yesterday I was thinking about soft Greek sands sipping pina coladas and getting my body ready to squeeze into a bikini and today I'm looking at my belly thinking I might as well eat; bring on the cream cakes as this is only going to get bigger.

I wake up in the middle of the night having a panic attack, thinking how useless I'm going to be as a mother. I can just about look after myself let alone a small human that is going to totally depend on me. I don't know anything about babies, only that they cry and poo a lot, I have never changed a baby's bum before and what way does the nappy even go? I lie there looking at Liam snoring away, thinking to myself how he's so calm. He hates having no sleep and from what I've gathered from friends is that you don't get a lot of sleep with babies. The one big thing they always do is bang on about how little sleep they've had. It's almost like a competition with them: 'Oh I can't tell you how tired I am, Max had me up 3 times last night and I feel like a walking zombie today' then the other comes out with, 'Oh I know how you feel, this little grotbag decided to play the piano at 2am this morning and wouldn't go back to bed until 4am.' They continue this conversation until one says, 'Oh you definitely win, bless you, is there anything we can do for you? Here, let us buy you another coffee, you need it.' I always just sit there quiet when these conversations come up as I don't want to rub in the fact that I've slept like a baby for 9 hours straight, which in itself is a stupid saying as from what I hear, they don't bloody sleep at all. Why is this saying still going? I reckon in the old days everyone used to drug their babies to get them to sleep with a little bit of whisky in their bottles. I wonder if that is still frowned upon.

Lying there awake, looking at my belly and wondering how I'm going to cope isn't going to get me very far; I just need to women up and get on with it. 12 weeks is the time you start to tell people as I think that's the safe zone. I think I'm going to have to tell certain people before that though as I'm not a great liar, they will just know by my face that something is up with me. I think I'll go see Smother, Dad and Louise tomorrow then that's it: that will be my circle of trust complete. Now to try and get some sleep which is easier said than done with SIR SNOREALOT lying next to me.

I awake from a deep sleep where I dreamt I was running away from something. I can remember thinking to myself that I wasn't running quickly enough, I had to run quicker when I suddenly go into the position of a chimpanzee and start with my hands on the ground, leaping myself though the air, pushing me forward, quicker, higher, faster. I could feel the air race across my skin as I got more height with every push I took, soaring though the streets of Rome on all fours, which is weird as I have never been to Rome. In the dream, I wonder why everyone doesn't run this way for it takes less effort and is so much quicker as I outrun the person I was trying to get away from and end up safe. WHAT IS WRONG

WITH ME? Who dreams stuff like this? I would like to say it's a one-off but it's not, it's a reoccurring dream I have at least once a week. Someone once mentioned about maybe taking myself to see a hypnotherapist as they seem to think I was a chimp in a former life? I mean it would make sense as I do like to groom other humans and I do get very protective over my friends and family so you could describe that as territorial. I also have a lot of facial expressions when communicating with human beings and the fact that I'm calling them human beings almost implies that I am not!

After feeling slightly concerned about the fact I am part chimp, I turn my focus on how shit I feel again; this growing a baby stuff is starting off not how I hoped. I'm looking at myself in the mirror, a pale yellow, sweaty mess with big bags under my eyes because I have been dreaming of running like a chimp. I DO NOT LOOK LIKE ANGELINA JOLIE, I LOOK MORE LIKE A HOBBIT!

Today I am working with Smother and I am going to try and find a quiet moment to tell her that she is going to be a nanny, awwwww, just thinking that is very sweet and makes me feel warm inside. I feel like I'm starting to get used to the idea of having a baby and I know I won't have to do it alone as I have such wonderful friends and family to help me when I am having a breakdown.

Walking into the salon, I am greeted by our lovely Tina who is our adorable apprentice. She looks like what I can only imagine Bambi would look like if it was in human form: big, brown, doughy eyes, massive eyelashes and perfect, natural hair - the type of hair that has the most perfect natural highlights running through and so thick and long it's almost like she has just walked of the set of a L'Oreal advert. It's quite annoying really that someone this young is just so beautiful. Oh yeah, Tina is only 19 and at that age, I still had a brace, my hair looked like a mushroom, my make-up skills were something else and that's not a good something else.

"Hi Soph"

"Oh hi Tina, how are you today Love?"

"I am fine Guess what I am going to a rave at the weekend im soooo excited."

"Why do you want to go to a rave, all you get at those things are hot sweaty people on drugs and weird music."

" I just want to try one so I can say I have been to a rave"

"mmmmmm ok well we will talk more about this situation later, How is my day looking today?"

"your busy but your first client is Mrs Trout"

Now . . . Mrs Trout is one of my favourite clients, one of my oldest clients and is just adorable but you would never know it; this Lady just oozes class and elegance. She would put any woman to shame, even now at her fragile age. I just adore listening to her stories about her life: in the golden years she was a hat model at a young age in the West End and it was there she then met her future husband who was from Sicily. She tells me her parents did not approve of their love because he was in the circus as a high wire artist so she rebelled and moved away with him to travel with the circus as the helping hand around the circus ring. This is where she fell in love with the elegance of aerial skills whereupon she asked to learn them so she could perform with her love in the show. Oh her stories go on and on and I could tell you them all day. For all I know her stories could be all fake but I don't care I get lost in them every time. I almost get upset when I have other clients in-between her as I just want to give her my undivided attention but unfortunately in this job you have to share yourself like a piece of pie for to many hungry clients. Sometimes I wish I was a cupcake as there is no sharing involved with a cup cake

- I mean who shares a cupcake right? Tina is still telling me who I have in when I hear Smother in the back kitchen making the morning tea, crashing and banging around until I hear her swear so I'm assuming she has spilt something, nothing new there. Now, do I tell her now about the baby or do I wait until after the day is done? Who am I kidding? AS if I can keep my mouth shut until later! So let's take a deep breath and go do this . . .

I walk into the back. "Morning Mum."

Smother jumps out of her skin, quite funny really but of course she doesn't think so.

"Oh Sophie, you frightened the living daylights out of me, why are you sneaking around like that?"

I deny I've been sneaking around anywhere! But she continues: "Anyway I'm glad you're here early even if you did nearly kill me off. I was talking to Ruth last evening and the conversation came up about you and Liam travelling to Greece and she told me something very frightening about the taxi drivers out there. Apparently, the wife of someone Ruth knows nearly got taken hostage if the husband didn't give the taxi driver what he wanted! So I DO NOT want you going anywhere in a taxi out there. You promise me as you are too precious to me to lose and I couldn't . . . "

"Mum, stop."

"NO Soph, I know you think I worry but you are my baby girl and when you have children you will understand."

"Well that's what I want to talk to you about. You see, I'm going to . . . have a baby."

Silence hit the room. You could cut the atmosphere with a knife which was not the response I thought Smother would give but this woman is unpredictable so I don't know why I keep trying to guess her moves.

"Mum, are you ok?"

"Em, yes darling, I am just processing the information you have given me . . . are you sure?"

"Why does everyone keep asking me that? Of course I'm sure Mum and I feel like poo everyday so yeah, pretty sure."

Smother starts welling up looking at me with her big magnified eyes.

"Oh darling, my baby girl is going to be a mummy! Are you ok? Does dad know?"

"I think so and no he doesn't so you can't tell him ill come round later and tell him with your there, I just couldn't work with you today and not say anything. I am a bit scared if I'm honest, nothing seems natural about any of this even though people say it is. I thought I was supposed to feel an overwhelming feeling of joy when I found out but instead, I feel very scared and that makes me question if I'm ready for this? Liam is really excited which almost makes me feel worse for feeling like this . . . oh Mum how am I going to bring up a child?"

"Come here darling, let me give my baby girl a cuddle and tell her everything is going to be ok, everything you are feeling is normal and actually is very good you're feeling like this. As you already know, it's going to be hard so you're going in with your eyes wide open but let me tell you, it's the best thing you will ever do as every day I wake up beaming with pride for you. I love you more than your ever know and I'll support you every step of the way, you will never be alone."

"Thanks Mum, it's going to be one loved baby with you about."

"AND IF ANYONE HURTS A SINGLE HAIR ON OUR BABY'S HEAD, NANNY WILL STAB THEM!"

"Mum, you can't go around stabbing people, what sort of lesson is that giving our child?"

"See, you're already acting like a mature mum but you know what I mean Soph, I will be a very protective Nanny . . . oh my, I am going to be a Nanny!"

That's when the flood gates open. Smother was squeezing me so tight, crying and kissing my head. I could feel tears in my freshly-washed hair but I'll let her off, she's happy and surprisingly, so am I.

"Sophie I'm telling you, no way on this earth are you going to Greece now. No arguments, I cannot deal with the panic I would be having all the time you are away so you're just going to have to have a holiday down the road in sunny Margate."

"Ok mum."

Isn't it crazy that Liam basically gave the same support as Smother did but somehow, I already feel calmer about the whole baby thing knowing my mum is there for me?

Work was a pleasure today, all my clients turned up on time. One of my lovely clients wanted a total restyle as she had just split up with her boyfriend and there is nothing better than making a newly single lady, through no fault of her own, feel good. You men are just total twats at times, let me tell you that if you think the grass is greener on the other side it's bound to be fake! Anyway, my client walked out of our salon feeling like Beyoncé, a strong independent women, whoop, whoop, you go girl! I really hope that grass that he left her for has been pissed on by a dog and is now turning yellow and dry.

Leaving work when it's dark sucks but nothing can dampen my mood this evening as I'm driving to the family home to tell Dad the good news and on the way I have changed things up in the music department. No Whitney tonight, I'm feeling Linkin Park is the way forward seeing as they always makes me feel pumped and ready to take on the world. I'm driving along head-banging and trying to growl/scream along to the song and thinking this moment in time would make the best Carpool T.V ever . . . James Corden, if you're reading this, I am free anytime, just send me a message.

Pulling up on Mum and Dad's drive, I take a moment to look at the house in the dark; it looks so warm and inviting. The lights are on inside, I can see they have the log fire going and just in that moment, like a flash, I'm taken back to my childhood growing up in this very house. My Mum has always had everything just so, dinner always cooked and on the table for Dad as he came home from work, kettle was always on, our pjs were always warming on the radiator and the house always smelt like fresh washing. Then there's my Dad he was and still is, my absolute hero, he is the real life Peter Pan. Nothing was too much trouble growing up with him around: if I wanted to make mud pies, he let me and if I wanted to stay up late, he let me even if Mum disagreed. I remember one sunny day I found a seagull's egg on the ground, convinced it was going to hatch. My dad got an old slipper, popped the egg inside then put the slipper in the airing cupboard to keep it warm, trying to trick the unborn chick that its mother was still caring for it. I checked on that egg every day for two months when one day my Dad broke the bad news to me that it wasn't going to hatch. I was so upset, in my head, I had visions of me and my pet seagull. WTF was I thinking, who wants a pet seagull? But my Dad, who knew that seagulls were absolute knob heads and the spawn of Satan, not ever once did he rain on my parade and tell me the truth about seagulls. All he saw was his little girl wanting to save wildlife, supporting me every step of the way. Even when I was in tears because it didn't hatch, he made me feel better by suggesting to take it into Show and

Tell at school and before that he had to blow out the inside of the egg so it didn't go rotten. Now that is a sight to see, your dad over the kitchen sink with a straw in one side of the egg trying not to get any of the contents inside his mouth. I hope Liam realises he has a lot to live up to, as in my opinion no one will ever be as amazing as my dad.

As I get closer to the front door I can hear Ozzy Osbourne blaring out of the house . . . yep, that's right, my Mum and Dad love Ozzy. I knock on the door, wait a second, no one comes, I knock again. I know they are in because I can hear Dad trying to sing/growl along to the song, so I patiently wait but still no answer. Jeez Dad, I think you need a hearing aid. I decide to take matters into my own hands and go round to the back to try the gate. Damn, it's locked so no other thing for it, I'm going to have to climb it. Many times have I climbed this gate when I was young so I can basically jump over it, simple. Em, maybe not so simple: I'm now stuck on the gate with fear rising inside and having visions of plummeting to my death over the other side. SHIT, SHIT, SHIT! What am I going to do? The music is too loud for them to hear and it's too dark for anyone to see me. Argh, that's it, I'm stuck here forever and I'm going to have to give birth on the top of this gate. What was I thinking being able to climb? I am a fully grown adult now, not a supple 10 year-old. Aha, my phone is in my pocket! Let's ring the house number. No answer. Seriously? Ok, let's try Liam . . .

"Hello."

"Hey babe, listen, I need your help, I'm stuck!"

"Stuck where?"

"On top of my parents gate"

"What?"

"I know, can you just come help me please? I think I'm getting a splinter in my foofoo."

"Soph, what? Why? Oh forget it, I don't want to even know. Yep ok, on my way."

"Thanks babe, please hurry."

Waiting for someone always feels like forever, especially when you're stuck on top of a gate. Little advice for anyone thinking of getting stuck: do it in the summer when your bum doesn't get cold or your legs don't get pins and needles. I actually think I have frost bite in my hands as I hear the choice of music change to Elvis Presley . . .

I can see Liam's van pulling up: my Hero is here.

"Soph, where are you?"

"Eh? Liam, look around."

Laughter erupts from his mouth.

"Yeah, it's hilarious, I know, now can you please help your wife down?"

"Yeah of course, but first, smile!"

Liam has his phone out of his pocket to take what he thinks to be an amusing picture of me . . . knob head. He lifts me down, trying to be gentle but actually it really hurt as he was squeezing that bit of skin on the back of your arms as he dragged me down.

Finally! Back down to a safe level and still hearing through triple glazed glass Mum singing like Tina Turner and Dad sounding like Rod Stewart, I try the door one more time. Nope. Nothing, so that's it, I'm done, I'm going home!

THURSDAY 1st November 2018

A new day is upon us: things to do, people to see and as I haven't got work this morning, I'm going to make it my mission to tell Dad once again our big news I just hope Smother can keep her mouth shut. I think I'll quickly pop to Louise's to tell her too.

It's no good, I think I just have to accept the fact I don't like tea anymore, I wonder why I've just gone off it? Today though, despite not liking tea, I think I feel slightly better, not so sick. I won't count my chickens yet though as smells are still making me gag. I'm struggling at work at the moment as the smell of perm lotion is really making me want to vom but it's not realistic in my job to pick and choose what you want to do so I just have to suck it up and not breathe too deep. Shallow breaths is the key, I'll do that until I pass out. I suppose.

11am, I turn up at Louise's house all excited at seeing them all, especially the new bubba. Quick, open the door, it's cuddle time!

Daniel opens the door looking horrendous.

"Wow Dan, are you ok, are you ill?"

"No, why?"

"Oh, no reason, how is it being a Dad to two?"

"Well if you like the training for the SAS then yeah I love it."

I didn't really know how to take that as he doesn't seem the type to like the SAS but you never know someone, I suppose. Anyway: "Is Lou in?"

"Yeah, she's in the lounge, go through."

The door to the lounge is pulled to and as I get closer I hear a strange noise coming from inside. I knock on the door very lightly as I don't want to wake anyone, I hear Louise calling me in. As I walk into the room, that weird noise is getting louder like a low humming, almost a vibrating hum. It keeps coming in waves of noise but the room is dark and I am struggling to see anything. Louise apologizes for it being so dark and pulls back a curtain from behind her sofa on which she is sitting. I have to blink twice because I can't quite believe what I'm seeing: Louise on the sofa crossed-legged, no top on and two suction caps attached to her nipples with pipes going from the suction caps leading down to two bottles which are placed either side of her legs. So this is where that weird humming noise is coming from. It's then I notice liquid draining down the pipes into the bottles.

"It's rude to stare Soph."

"What? Oh sorry but what the hell am I witnessing here????" Louise is giggling away whist eating a Snickers bar.

"They are breast pumps Soph, I'm expressing milk for Hugo and this is the easiest way, plus they can be hands-free if you position the cushions right."

I walk closer, to get a better look if I'm honest . . .

"WOW! Your nipples are huge, they look like udders . . . actually come to think of it, this scene does remind me of a cow being milked by a machine."

Louise gives me a look.

"Does everyone do this when they have had a baby?"

"It depends on how you want to feed your baby. Sit down Soph and stop staring, you're making me nervous."

"You're nervous? I'm the one that should be nervous."

"Why?"

"Well, I have something to tell you . . . em . . . er . . ."

"Oh come on, Soph! Loose Women starts soon, spit it out!"

"Ok, I'm pregnant."

Louise obviously moves too quickly as one of those cup things come flying off her nipple and boob milk hits her in the eye.

"You're what?"

"Yep, I'm preggers, up the duff, bun in the oven, knocked up."

"Bloody hell, what have you done that for? Have you seen me? Take a good look - hair hasn't been washed in a week, I have baby shit on my leggings, I still have to wee in the bath as my fanny is so swollen and sore and I haven't slept in ten days straight!"

"Ok, so it's a blast then. I don't know why I came to tell you, it's not like I'm scared or anything."

"Oh Soph, I'm so sorry. Don't listen to me, I'm just being a bitch and it's your first so it's fine, you will get some sleep, come here."

Louise opens her arms to offer a hug which I refuse as her nipple is still leaking and I don't want boob juice on me.

I stay for an hour to have snuggles with Hugo and have toy dinosaurs thrown at my head by Felix the sibling who's such a lovely boy. He is probably feeling a little pushed out by Hugo coming along, not that you would know seeing I only witnessed him try to smother him twice whilst I was there. Oh well, I'm sure he will calm down.

I get in my car and wave goodbye to Louise and Daniel who are standing in their door way looking like victims of Zombie Apocalypse. I'm trying not to think too deeply about what mess I have got myself into . . . stop it Soph, you were really happy this morning before you saw the joy police. Yeah but Louise is the real deal, this is what life is going to be like! Did you see her hair? I know I tell people washing your hair too often is bad for you but Christ I thought she had dunked her head in a chip fat fryer . . . I don't want my hair like that . . . and you won't, Smother will do it for us . . . you're right, it's going to be ok, my hair will be clean and I won't have boob juice all over me, thanks again to the calming side of my brain.

In the salon Smother gives me a huge hug as I walk in and quizzes me on where I was last night. I tried to explain but she was being weirder than usual, so I decide to leave it but as I walk through the salon the clients are smiling at me but also staring. Why is everyone being weird???? I look back at Smother who is in reception, she has a mischievous manner about her. She's bloody told them, I know she has! I haven't even seen the doctor or a midwife yet and she has told at least three people and that's in here - I wonder who she has been on the phone too as well.

"Mum, can I have a word please?"

"Yes darling, what's wrong?"

"You've told them haven't you?"

"Told them what?"

"Don't play dumb, Mother."

"Oh well, I was so excited and it just sort of slipped out."

"I haven't even told dad yet!"

"yes well I was expecting to see you last night?"

"Well I tried but you both had Ozzy playing and, oh it doesn't matter, the thing that matters is that three ladies know before family, Mum, it's not on."

"I'm sorry, I promise I won't tell another soul."

"Who else have you told?"

"No-one . . ."

"Mum?"

"Only Nan, that's all."

"Great, so now half of the world knows if Nan knows… hang on you told Nan and not dad?"

"You told me not to tell Dad"

"I assumed you wouldn't tell anyone Mum, promise me you wont tell anyone else"

"I promise, cross my heart and hope to die. Well obviously I don't hope to die very much - the opposite! What a silly saying, I take it back, I just promise."

"Ok , thank you."

It's four o'clock and Dad pops into the salon which is weird, he never pops into the salon, something is wrong. I excuse myself from my client and go to see dad, his face tells me he's angry. As well as angry, he also looks like he has just stepped out of a boy band, wearing super-tight skinny jeans, boat shoes and a top on with a cowl neckline. On the front of it there's a picture of a guitar and his hair has so much gel in it, it looks wet. Why would you want your hair to look that wet? But what do I know I am only a hairdresser.

"Hi Dad, are you ok?"

"Yes, are you?"

"Yeah I'm fine, what brings you here?"

"You tell me?"

"I don't know Dad, you're the one that has walked through the door."

"Yes and I wonder why that is Sophie."

Oooooh, he called me Sophie, it's bad, he never calls me that . . .

"Oh Dad, please tell me what's wrong."

"Well I spoke with Nan this morning and she had some very interesting news for me."

See? I knew it, the whole world knows!

"Dad, I came to the house last night but you had Ozzy then Elvis playing and you both didn't hear me at the door. Great singing by the way. I did try to get round the back but the gate won, I got stuck but I did try I promise, I tried really hard in fact."

"Really, you came round?"

"Yeah I did, I stayed for quite a while too."

With that, Dad just pulls me into his big bear arms and gives me the biggest and tightest hug ever - I think I'm going to pass out. In fact, I have to tap out: he always taught me and my bro when fighting that if it ever got too much we had to tap out and the other was to let go straight away otherwise if we didn't we would pay for it one way or another. Smother comes bounding through the salon to greet Dad.

"Did you know about this Jackie?"

"yes but Sophie promised me not to tell you"

"You told your mum though?"

"Well yes but she is old and I wanted to give her reason to keep on living"

"Don't give me that shit Jackie you just couldn't keep your mouth shut"

"How very dare you"

Luckily, a client was waiting to come through the door so the argument stopped sharpish.

"Was lovely to see you Dad I will ring you later on" Dad leaves the salon and I whisper to mum that she is in trouble as I don't think that row is over.

CHAPTER SEVEN

MANY DOCTORS

SATURDAY 17TH NOVEMBER 2018

Today is the day we meet the midwife, I'm so excited as this almost makes it real. I'm not just pretending to be pregnant even though I know I def am as my boobs are growing at a pace quicker than the speed of light. I have always wanted bigger boobs, I keep looking down thinking of how I'm definitely having a boob job after this whole pregnancy thing is over. I just look better when they are not two fried eggs and more like small oranges. I actually need a proper bra, not just a training one. Liam is loving them, I keep catching him looking at me in a way he hasn't before but I can tell you all now that is all he is doing as OH MY GOD they hurt - even having the spray from the shower head hurts them so no way am I having anyone squeeze them especially not with his rough hands. It would be like sandpaper groping your boobs, NO THANK YOU!

There's a knock at the door.

"Liam she is here."

"Ok I'm just coming"

I open the door, "Hi can I help you?"

"Yes hopefully I'm looking for Sophie"

"Yes this is me, what can I help you with?"

"I'm your assigned midwife Mark, nice to meet you."

"Oh you're a midwife! Sorry I thought you were selling something, so sorry, please come in. You don't look like a midwife."

"I know, I get that a lot because I'm a man, there aren't many of us about in this profession."

Liam walks into the living room looking confused but before I have a chance to explain, Mark has already got up from the sofa and put his hand out for Liam to shake, introducing himself. Wow I didn't realise how small Liam is as Mark is towering above him looking down on him. Liam is now pushing out his chest, peacocking I think you call it.

As we take a seat Mark says, "If you are not comfortable with me being your midwife because I am a man I totally understand, you will not be the first to want the change to another midwife. Please don't feel pressured or in any way uncomfortable, I came into this profession fully aware it is not the normal career choice for most men. I also understand this is one of the biggest, scariest time in a woman's life, you both need to be comfortable with me being here."

"I am absolutely fine with it Mark, I personally think it's wonderful you've taken on this profession, it's about time in our day and age. Why should it just be a women's profession? We have male doctors, so not much difference, don't you agree Liam?"

"Em . . . yeah."

I didn't realise how many forms you have to fill in when having a baby, it's like doing a C.V. They want to know the ins and outs of a duck's arse, like what blood group you are . . . I mean, who bloody knows that???? If you have HIV, if you are smoking crack, if Liam is knocking me about, have you any mental health issues, what job you do, whether you have people around you to support you, it's all there. Liam is very silent through all of this and he keeps staring at Mark. I know that look, he's angry and I can see the pulse in his forehead going - not quite sure why he is angry but I'm sure I'll find out later. Mark asks me to stand up so he can measure me . . . why I need to be measured I don't know for it's not like you're going to get any taller through the pregnancy but hey ho, he then gets out blood vial pots . . .

"Em, what are they for?"

"I need to take some samples of blood from you to check a number of things like your blood group and whether you have HIV, hepatitis or syphilis, whether you're anaemic and lastly if you have a blood condition such as sickle cell anaemia or thalassaemia."

For some reason I did not prepare myself for blood tests, oh Jesus, why didn't I prepare my mind? Ok Soph, pull yourself together, it's going to be okay, Liam is here, he will help.

"Em, the thing is Mark, I'm a bit of a wimp when it comes to things like blood."

Mark laughs: wow, his laugh is deep, I can feel it vibrate in my belly.

"Please don't worry, I have many women not good with blood. Would you prefer I take it whilst you lay down? I can do it on the sofa if you want?"

Liam is now watching Mark gently put a pillow under my head, Liam decides to get up to sit with me on the sofa. I'm now laying there looking up at two men looking down on me . . . well, this is a first. Mark takes my arm gently, his hands are so soft. Liam is stroking my forehead, his hands are so rough but it's quite nice to have all this attention then I hear Mark's voice.

"All done, well done, you didn't pass out."

"That's incredible, I didn't even feel you do anything, you're amazing!" Liam gives me a glare, I honestly don't know what goes through men's mind; here I am having blood taken for every disease under the sun and he thinks I'm bloody flirting with the midwife, typical!

We say our goodbyes to Mark then as soon as we shut the door Liam pipes up with, "Don't you think it's a bit weird, a man wanting to be a midwife? Bet he's gay, I did catch him eyeing me up at one point. I mean, who can blame him? Look at me, I'm an Adonis. I wonder how many men he has stolen from their wives, you better watch out babe, you have competition."

He then turns away from me doing a funny walk and flicking his hair . . . what a KNOB!

SUNDAY 18TH NOVEMBER 2018

I'm going out for the day with Louise and her brood today to the zoo and I'm really looking forward to it. I have missed Louise since she has been a constant milking machine to her new edition but she rang me up saying she has cabin fever and needed to get out the house as Daniel was driving her mad.

So we arrive at the zoo and the first thing I notice is that it stinks, I'm sure it didn't smell this bad before. Christ, what is that????

Louise picks up Hugo to smell him and yep, it was his arse.

"Jesus LOUISE, what are you feeding him? That stinks!" Louise just glares at me, you know I think it's a mum thing, that glare. I call it the Death Stare; all mums seem to have it. I've been observing them closely since finding out and it looks to me that the trick is to turn your head quickly in the direction you want to give the Death Stare then open your eyes really wide, slightly jutting out your chin. You then stay completely still and stare without blinking. Somehow the small ones seem to know this stare and take notice, complying with what you want them to do, like I am with Louise as I say sorry and scamper away.

The zoo is nice if a bit cold but it's great catching up with Lou. She also gives me pointers on what to expect whilst pregnant and I've got to say it all sounds delightful. Why do so many women do this? I've got so much to look forward to. Friends, what would you do without them? Hey, they're always there to tell you the truth, no fluffy clouds to go with it.

Whilst trying to stop Felix from climbing through the fence because he wanted to stroke the monkeys, I receive a phone call from Mark asking me if I could get to the hospital the next day for our first scan and also to let me know all my blood tests came back normal. He says he doesn't normally phone through appointments, it was just there was a cancellation in the scanning department so he wanted me to have it. Awwwww bless him, I think I'm going to really like Mark looking after me, he seems a very caring guy plus it gives Liam a little lift to think someone fancies him.

Louise is sitting at the café table feeding Hugo when a women walks past, looks over to her and huffs as if she is doing something wrong. Louise glares up in her direction and yells, "DO YOU WANNA PICTURE LUV? IT WILL LAST LONGER." Oooooohhhhh this lady picked on the wrong women to huff at. If there is anything I have learned about post-pregnant women DO NOT stare or have an opinion about their parenting choices. They will go straight for the jugular, toss you around like a rag doll and spit you out only picking you back up to swallow you whole whilst then regurgitating it for their children to eat. Personally, I'd rather take my chances in the lion's enclosure.

"Who does that twat of a woman think she is? If I didn't have Hugo latched on, I'd have had that woman over this bench just to pull her knickers down to embarrass her; it makes me so fucking mad that people think It's inappropriate to breast feed your baby in public."

"Mummy, what does fucking mean?"

"Oh no, did I say that out loud Soph?"

"Errr . . . yeah you did."

"Oh no! Ok, damage control: well Felix, Mummy shouldn't have said that word, it is very naughty and you should never say that word again, ok?"

"Ok Mummy, can I have an ice cream please, a Smartie one?"

"Soph, get Felix an ice cream please, whilst I calm down and concentrate on Hugo."

"Sure, do you want one? I don't think the zoo sells gin so will a Magnum do?" Louise laughs. "Yes please."

MONDAY 19TH NOVEMBER 2018

Getting myself ready to go to the hospital for our first scan I catch my reflection in the mirror and I'm definitely getting bigger but I'm at that awkward fat stage. I don't look like I'm pregnant, I just look like I've eaten too many pies! I have noticed at work the clients have been looking whilst I've been doing their hair. I know they think it but not one has had the courage to ask if I'm pregnant. I just look a bit chubby, I'm going with the choice of leggings and a long top today: easy access to see our baby, eeeeeeeek, it's exciting.

"Liam, are you ready to go?" He was on the phone when I walked in the living room and jumped out of his skin - why do I have this effect on people? I must be like a ninja: silent, deadly, almost invisible.

"I have got to go, I'll call you back later."

"Who was that?"

"It was Paul wanting to go to snooker later."

"Oh ok, you ready?"

"Yeah let's go."

The car journey to the hospital is silent which is strange because I thought both of us would be excited. Maybe we are both a little nervous as when we see that little image on screen, I think it will become more real. Sitting in the waiting room watching all these pregnant women go in and out of different rooms I see some look glowing and some just look angry at life. I really hope I get to look like the glowing ones.

Something no one tells you about is how cold that jelly stuff is that they squeeze all over your belly and I'm so ticklish that as soon as a drop of it hits my belly I'm giggling like a little school girl. Liam is there holding my hand looking nervous as the sonographer keeps pushing this hand-held scan thing over my belly, she must have gone over the area 5 times.

"I knew it, I'm not pregnant am I? I'm so sorry for wasting your time." The sonographer looks at me with confused eyes then smiles.

"You're certainly pregnant, in fact you're a little further gone than you think - you are in fact 4 months pregnant instead of 3."

She swings the screen round for us to see and wow, there on the screen is our baby just swimming around. "Its legs look really skinny and its head looks massive, is that normal?"

Yes, she tells me, laughing. Why is she laughing, is she laughing at our unborn child?

"Everything is normal, looking very healthy, so please don't be scared or worry about the skinniness of your baby's legs. They will soon fill out with all that good nutrition you're filling yourself with to feed your baby."

Liam is looking at me smiling, also judging me because I have eaten half of the stock of KFC Chicken Royales but chicken is protein, right? The sonographer gives us pictures to take away with us of our little chicken look-alike baby but I can tell you this: when I saw that heartbeat and its squashed up little nose, I fell in love in an instant. I couldn't care what my baby looks like as its been made by us/me more. I think as I'm still growing it what's Liam doing now? Nothing. So I would like most of the praise please.

CHAPTER EIGHT

WEEKEND AWAY

FRIDAY 23rd NOVEMBER 2018

Liam and Paul are going away on a lads' weekend this week which will be nice for them, give them a bit of bonding time. They are going paintballing then out somewhere in Brighton. If they weren't going paintballing I might be questioning again their relationship as Brighton is flying the gay flag very high and very proud but I don't think many gay guys like balls flying at them at 30mph . . . oh hang on, I just reread my thought process. Of course they would, I do often question what would I rather have . . . . to find out my husband is having an affair with a woman or to find out it's with a man and I think I would rather a man as I know then it wouldn't be my fault. I just haven't got a four o' clock shadow or a penis. Saying goodbye to Liam is always a bit hard because one part of me knows I'll miss him but the other part of me thinks of how much crap telly I can watch without him butting in telling me how utter shit it is. Also I get the whole bed to myself to starfish on so the only downside is the fact I will have to feed Psycho Cat. I did buy myself one of those grabber things so I won't need to bend down to its level otherwise it will know I am vulnerable bent down and go for the kill. Probably give me sepsis with its bite and I am far too busy this weekend to get sepsis!

SATURDAY 24th NOVEMBER 2018

I have wedding hair to do today which I always get nervous about as it's such pressure to have to make someone look and feel stunning on their big day but it's ok as I have Kate helping me. She is one of our stylists and is utterly fabulous at her job. The problem with being pregnant is that you're just so damn emotional, it's ridiculous. I cried last night because of the advert that shows a donkey walking up a hill with its back loaded with far too much and they had the voiceover as if the donkey was speaking begging to please help it: 'I'm too old to carry all my owner's water butts, please just spare £5 a month to help others like me and help my owners get a water pump installed at the bottom of the mountain so we can graze peacefully in our old age.' I mean, Christ, first of all, this donkey looked and talked like Eeyore; that would be enough to push any pregnant woman over the edge and secondly, why do they then need to add an image of a sad looking child stroking its lifelong friend Eeyore dying at the side of the road? Well, all I can say is well done Mr Charity Advert Man, you certainly got me. Not only was I a blubbering mess, I am now signed up for a year paying not 5 but £10 a month as I want to save them all! What I am actually saying is, if a talking donkey is making me cry then I have no hope with any sort of emotional day especially a wedding!

Kate and I arrive at the wedding venue. I let Kate set up whilst I eat a selection of cold meats - I am finding if I don't have my meat dosage for the day I'm a right Diva and no one needs that today. Finished with my meats, I go wait with Kate for the wedding party to arrive. I have the bride to do so no pressure . . . why are my eyes welling up? Nothing has even happened. Oh come on Soph pull yourself together, breathe. I take in a deep breath, count to ten and the bride is here. First thing with wedding hair is you prep with dry shampoo: this stuff should be your best friend. It gives the hair texture and volume which is perfect for backcombing. It's all going swimmingly well, the bride is coming together - well her hair is. I think she is drunk already and its only 11am for she is telling me she loves me which in my eyes is a clear sign of being drunk. The bridesmaids are taking her glass off her which is another sure sign. So what though? It's her day and if she wants to be wasted on her big day I say let her bring on the Sambucas . . . maybe this is why I've never been bridesmaid? Just putting the finishing touches to the hair when something feels weird in my belly like I have butterflies in there . . . maybe it's all that cheese I ate? Ooooh no, it's definitely something else because there it is again, only this time a bit stronger. It makes me feel a little nauseous actually, like something is flipping around in there. OMG, IT'S MY BABY, I CAN FEEL MY BABY! Not sure I like it but I'm crying again so I must like it.

The bride is looking at me worried: "Are you ok?"

"Oh I'm so sorry, yes I'm pregnant and I just felt my baby move for the first time."

"Omg, congratulations!" At this point she swings round on her chair and just hugs my belly saying it was the best wedding present ever which I gotta say I kinda agree: what a happy day this is turning out to be!

Hair is done and she looks beautiful. In the end my bride went for a very romantic style which in the eyes of the public looks like it has been thrown up in a very easy natural way but let me tell you these type of hairstyles are often the hardest. You want them to look natural, even with a few strands of hair draping down effortlessly, but every part has got to be secured in such a way it's going to last all day without the bride at some point looking like she has been pulled through a hedge backwards. As I begin to show her the back of her hair I 'm proudly smiling because it looks so goddamn beautiful then she suddenly comes out with, "Oh we nearly forgot my veil" looking to one of her bridesmaids to go fetch it. Chief bridesmaid returns to the room with which can only be described as Princess Diana's veil: about 10metres long and extremely heavy. I think I'm going to have a breakdown. Little tip for all you brides out there: to present your veil to your hairdresser on the day of the wedding when the week before you were adamant you weren't having one . . . well, how do I say this politely? Nope, there is no polite way, let's just say you're a bit dickish even if it is your special day! The problem we hairdressers have with this is that we create the style sometimes around the veil if we knew we had one so now what I have is a situation where this delicate hairstyle is going to be dragged down due the utter length of the veil and now I WANT TO CRY AGAIN.

I am just staring at it, not moving and the bride has tears in her eyes too. I am guessing we are not welling up at the same thing as my tears are turning angry and her tears look like happy tears. I'm assuming she thinks I am happy too but I take a look at my face in the mirror because I am standing behind her and I can tell you now my face didn't get the memo to be happy. I excuse myself from the room to try and compose myself in the bathroom before I make some rash decision to kill her. I really don't want to have my baby in prison, I have watched documentaries on that type of thing and it's not pretty. I take ten big deep breaths, redo my hair and hold my head up high as I go back in. I see Kate give me the eye through the mirror; we both know what we are thinking but we're professional so we quickly look away from each other's glance and get on with the job in hand. As

I am attaching the veil to the head I have to be a little rough with the comb to position it in place. The bride squirms slightly in her chair so I apologise to her and carry on when she says, "Oh it's quite heavy, isn't it?"

"Yes, this one is, did you have extra weights sewn into it for a neck workout?" She laughs but I don't think it's that funny as it really is heavy: I'm surprised her neck muscles have held out so far. Anyway, it's now in. I have probably attached the comb directly into her scalp but as they say, no pain, no gain, especially for brides. Kate is finished too and is necking Prosecco straight from the bottle. That is one downside of pregnancy, not drinking, it's frowned upon, apparently. When the bridal party leave the room, Kate and I both sigh and flop onto the bed. Lying next to each other we begin to giggle for no reason other than the fact we are both relieved I didn't murder anyone today, winning at holding my shit together.

I arrive home excited to have the house to myself. I jump in the bath, splash about a bit, get out, put my pjs on, draw the curtains and commence eating my way through the whole selection of Krispy Kreme doughnuts. I need to draw the curtains for this as no one needs to see me inhale 6 doughnuts at a time. Lying on the sofa I'm watching the whole saga of Twilight. I am obsessed with vampires and werewolves: when did they get so sexy? If I were Bella, I would have issues too. Poor girl, having to choose between a mysterious vampire and a hungry hormone-driven werewolf. If only life was like that, such a tough but beautiful predicament to be in.

SUNDAY . . . THE DAY AFTER THE DAY BEFORE

I wake up early to find drunken texts off my husband from the night before saying, 1. I'm so lucky to have you I lov eou seet dreamss, 2. where ar yu and 3. meet me bak at rom

I'm guessing 2-3 weren't meant for me, obviously Liam has misplaced Paul on their drunken night out. I glance at the time, it's only 8.15, a bit early to try and call him or is it? I'm just so excited to tell him I felt the baby move so ok, I'm going to try. It's just gone straight to answer phone, oh well it can wait.

I look down at my expanding belly and Psycho Cat looks up at me, he has taking a liking to my belly. He is just laying across it purring, stopping every now and then to look at me with an evil glance. I think this cat has imprinted on my unborn child as he still obviously still hates me but my belly he loves but then I've probably been watching too much Twilight.

1pm: my phone rings and it's Mark wanting to book in my next appointment but as I look through my diary for work, I just can't seem to find a space. I ask him what this appointment entails and he tells me it's just listening to baby's heart beat and measuring my bump. The question is, has he got a big enough tape measure because I am growing at the speed of light, this baby is going to be huge. We come to an arrangement of Mark visiting the salon one day next week so he can measure my orangutan belly there, then Smother can meet Mark and I can warn him of her passing out at any given moment so he can get used to her before the big day.

I suddenly realise what day it is.

"It's Sunday Mark, what are you doing working?"

"Babies don't know that it's Sunday, I have just finished a shift at the hospital."

"Well I hope you're going home to rest now?"

"Unfortunately not, my partner has arranged a lunch at our house so I have to go peel potatoes and pretend to be sociable to people we see twice a year."

"Oh well, I'm sure when you get home you'll enjoy every moment, sometimes the thought is worse than the actual event."

"I suppose you're right, I'll let you know when I see you, anyway I hope you're resting, you're the one having a baby."

"I am actually. Liam is away on a boy's weekend so I have the telly to myself. Oh and whilst you're on the phone, can cats imprint on your unborn child?"

Mark laughs loudly. "I'm guessing you have been watching Twilight right?"

"Err no, it's just our psycho cat won't leave my belly alone, he hates me as a person but my belly he likes."

"It's warm, that's why, you have your own central heating system going on in your stomach, the cat just likes the warmth."

"Oh great, I'm thinking we may have issues when the baby is born."

"Ha ha, no, don't panic, it will go straight back to hating you once the baby comes out."

"Thanks."

"You're welcome, enjoy your alone time whilst you can."

"I will and you enjoy your luncheon."

Weird . . . how did he know I've been watching Twilight? As I put down the phone, Liam walks through the door looking like shit.

"Hey, how was your night?"

"It was ok thanks, actually not that great to be honest. I really missed you."

"Awwww, cute. Sorry you didn't have a great time. Your texts came across different though, you were very drunk and your words were all over the place."

"Err, my texts?"

"Yeah, your texts"

"Well, what did I say?"

"Oh the norm . . . oh and I think a couple of them weren't meant for me."

"Why, what do you mean?"

"Well did you lose someone?"

"Err I dunno, I can't remember."

"Sounds like a good night."

"What did they say?"

"Oh nothing, don't worry"

"Ok, you sure?"

"Yeah I can cope with a couple of drunk texts, anyway I have something amazing to tell you . . . I felt the baby move yesterday!"

"What, are you kidding?"

"Nope, it's the weirdest feeling, it's like I have a bunch of butterflies in my belly flapping around!"

"This is fantastic news!" Liam walks over for a hug and I can smell him coming. I do hug him but I turn my head to the window I have open in the hallway. I mean, I don't want to be rude but he stinks.

CHAPTER NINE

ALL THE CONTACT

Another week has passed and I've noticed I'm getting more and more agitated as the weeks go on; either I'm losing my patience more often because of the pregnancy or more and more of the general public are turning into absolute morons, I am hoping the first because I cannot bring this baby into a world full of dickheads, excuse my French.

What I have noticed is that no one respects your personal space anymore - when did it suddenly become acceptable to touch a complete stranger's stomach?

Shopping for food the other day, a middle-aged woman, who at the time was bent over picking up a punnet of strawberries, noticed my protruding stomach above her and as she was standing back up, she just stroked my stomach and commented, "Oh how lovely, congratulations, when is it due?" She stood by her trolley waiting for my reply. Many things went through my mind in that split second, I'll let you in on a couple:

1. What the Hell is happening right now?
2. Do I actually know this women? Have I just erased her from my brain database due to my pregnant state?
3. Is she a witch?
4. Is this woman going to harm me and my baby?
5. Do I give her a swift punch in the throat?

6. Am I being a horrible bitch?

So once I had quickly processed all these questions, my brain suddenly lets me know I am still just standing there just staring at her. I quickly apologise and answer her innocent friendly question, whereupon she smiles and carries on with her shopping. I am left walking up and down the aisles still in shock asking myself if that's normal behaviour and have I got more of this touching stuff to come in which case should I get my belly a protective layer like a stab vest?

Since my food shop I have realised that yep, the touching stuff is happening a lot more.

When working, I have noticed clients, as they walk past me, have taken to either cuddling my bump from behind whilst I'm still blow-drying or just giving it a gentle tap or on the odd occasion they bend down to my belly to say hello. I am still adjusting to this strange human behaviour but slowly getting used to it. So buckle up ladies, prepare to be touched a lot.

Louise is coming into the salon today to get her hair done. I think it's the first time away from the kids in a while so I am getting everything ready to give her a pamper session. Tina comes onto the back room of the salon to let me know Louise is here so as I poke my head around the door to say hello, I notice the hay stack she has bundled up on the top of her head which she calls hair. What the hell has she been doing to it? It looks horrific: her roots are half way down her head, her ends look like a rat has been chewing on them and I don't think it has seen conditioner in a very long time. Louise was only booked in for a cut and blow-dry but there is no way I can send her out with roots like those. I ask Tina to gown her up and position her at the colouring station. Taking matters into my own hands, I text Daniel to tell him she's going to be a while and to get the expressed milk out of the fridge ready for Hugo's next feed. His reply was along the lines of how long she was going to be! I replied… however long it takes me to make his beautiful wife beautiful again, to be prepared to be wowed when she returns and to make sure he tells her she is beautiful and not to use none of his stupid jokes like she looks like He Man. His reply was just a simple agreement.

I go out to the salon to tell Louise not to worry, I've texted Daniel and told him to hold down the fort until her return, with that she just looks at me and begins to cry.

"Oh I'm sorry Louise, I thought I would treat you to get your hair done all nice again."

"No it's not that I'm sad, I'm actually ecstatically happy right now, do you know how long it's been since I have had anything like this done?"

"Well looking at your roots, I could hazard a guess luv." Louise is still crying but laughing at the same time. To be honest, she is sounding a bit hysterical now, she can't seem to control herself and her head is bent so far back, her mouth is wide open and she is cackling away. Wow, not only do you seem to get no sleep when having babies, they seem to send you temporally insane too. Jeez Louise, where's my tranquiliser gun when I need it?

Louise takes down her hair and tells me to be careful as it's disgusting and yep, the hair actually stays as if it still has a hairband in, it doesn't move. I begin the long process of beautifying my bestie. We begin with Balayage Technique as this is a low maintenance colour style for anyone that wants to look effortlessly goddamn gorgeous at all times. Louise's hair is just sucking up all the colour I'm putting on which tells me it needs a deep conditioning treatment. The conversation goes like this: Louise, what shampoo have you been using on your hair? Oh, just a cheap one that smells lush, why? Your hair is yelling at me to help it, that's why, I'm your best mate, just text me and tell me you need shampoo and conditioner will you? Ok sorry, didn't think you would get your knickers in a twist over shampoo, you're my walking advert at the end of the day and you may as well be using washing up liquid on your hair. Oh I did do that the other week. Again, the cackles start.

At the basin I ask Tina to put on our pure Keratin conditioning treatment on Louise's hair and ask her to leave it on for ten minutes, I mean it could do with being left on her hair for a about a month but I haven't got time for that so ten minutes will have to do.

Mark walks into the salon and Louise lifts her head out of the basin, looks towards the door and makes this weird meow noise. She then swings her head to look at me with her tongue halfway out of her head and mutters, "Who is that fine specimen of a man in reception?"

"That is my midwife Louise, put your tongue back in your mouth." Tina drags Louise's head back into the basin whilst I go to see Mark.

I waddle up to the reception area to rescue Mark from all the old ladies making a beeline for him, one has already got her claws into him asking if he could carry her shopping out to the car for her as she is soooooo weak and old which of course wouldn't bother me if she was actually weak and old. When this 'old frail woman' came into the salon only an hour previously, she was practically skipping down the salon showing Tina how she could still touch her toes, "So it's all down to yoga my dear, that's why I'm still so flexible and young at heart, you won't catch me asking for any help soon, you know if you don't use it you lose it my dear." Hmmmm, funny that you've suddenly lost it within

40 minutes of being in the salon. I am not going to be rude though, let her have her fun. I actually think Mark likes all the attention, I mean what gay guy doesn't but they are not to know that and neither does Louise so I'll let her make a fool of herself too. Cruel I know but I'm fat and hot so let me have a little fun.

Mark returns back into the salon looking red-faced.

"What do these ladies keep in their bags? It was like carrying solid gold bars out to the taxis."

"Yes sorry about that, they do tend to bring all their worldly belongings to the hairdressers, shall we go into the back Kitchen to check Bubba?"

"Wherever you're most comfortable Soph." I begin to laugh after he said comfortable. "What's that nowadays?" And the problem is I know it's only going to get worse. I move the Back kitchen chairs out of the way so I can lay down on the floor and that's when Mark looks at me strangely.

"What are you doing Soph?"

"Laying down, that's the position you need me, right?"

"Err yeah but I thought you had something proper to lay on rather than a hard floor, are you going to be ok down there?" I chuckle to myself and reply, "Yes, I'll be fine, I'm only pregnant and I'm not the size of a house yet, but it won't be long until I am, I know."

"Ok, as long as you're sure, let's get started." Mark gets all his equipment out that he needs then squeezes that horrible jelly stuff over my belly, I don't know why but it always makes me feel sick as he pushes it all around my skin with that little stick-listening thing. I don't know the technical name for it but you know sort of what I mean, right? Mark is still trying to find the heartbeat as all we can hear is a weird, whooshing, white noise when suddenly we catch a glimpse of the sound of what sounds like a train racing along. He looks down at me and smiles, "There he or she is sounding very healthy indeed, with a very strong and loud heartbeat." With that, I hear the salon go silent: no hairdryers are drying, no one is talking, it is just silent. All you can hear is my baby's heartbeat which brings a tear to my eye as I still can't believe how in love I am with this little heartbeat already. I'm lying on a kitchen floor with a towel as a pillow listening to my baby, life can't get much better than this - well I say that, a bed would probably be better plus an actual pillow rather than a towel but it's nearly perfect so I'll take it.

CHAPTER TEN

PSYCHICS

SATURDAY 8th DECEMBER 2018

Going out baby shopping with Smother today: eeeeeeeeeek, it's a very exciting day. I leap out of bed – well, I say leap but what I actually mean is I slowly roll and fall, managing just in time to swing my legs underneath me to support my weight. In my head though, I am a gazelle leaping with ease through life. So here I am up drinking tea while Liam is still in the land of zzzzzs as it is only 7.30. Looking into the garden there are signs it's going to be a beautiful day: the sun is shining, there is a dewy frost glistening brightly on the grass. I'm almost hypnotised at the day's beauty but suddenly, Psycho Cat falls off the top of the fence landing on the grass with a thump. The reason for the huge thump is because it has a present for me - another pigeon. He locks his gaze onto me like a predator stalking its prey, slowly moving up the garden dragging the pigeon towards the house. I can hear him meowing through our triple-glazed glass when I move towards the cat flap to lock it and hear the doorbell ring. Who can that be at this time in the morning? Please don't let it be the cat, it wouldn't surprise me if it knows my every move now and has upped his game by learning to jump and ring the bell. Cautiously, I move towards the door and decide to take a detour into the lounge to peek through the curtains and see Smother's face smiling at me from the other side of the glass. She is also holding up croissants so I decide to let her in as I'm starving. The door has only been opened an inch before she barges her way past me and heads towards the kitchen. "Morning mum, are you ok? Do you know what time it is?"

"Ha ha, of course I do dear . . ." but before she could finish her sentence, I hear her screaming a scream I have never heard before: a blood curdling one! I am now rushing towards the kitchen when I see why she is screaming. I begin to scream too when Liam comes flying down the stairs screaming with his fists at the ready. Not knowing what is going on, he looks at Smother who has blood spattered all over her. The kitchen is also covered in blood and I'm in the hallway nearly crying when suddenly something is flying towards my head. Liam jumps in the way to take the blow of the flying object which hits him in the face and drops to the floor. I have my hands covering my eyes peeking through the cracks of my fingers when it is suddenly silent. All I can hear is heavy breathing and Liam moaning about how his face hurts. I slowly take my hands away and look towards the floor; there on the floor is a pigeon, a now dead pigeon. I look up into the kitchen to see Smother standing in shock not knowing what to do or say, just looking around our kitchen at the devastation with pigeon blood dripping from her forehead. I notice Psycho Cat sitting on top of the kitchen worktop licking his paws and purring deeply like a freight train. Liam rushes past me and Mum to grab the cat off the side to chuck him outside, locks the cat flap and calls the cat a fucking dickhead who he's going to kill or take him to a rehoming centre. He is still muttering swear words under his breath as he walks towards me holding out his arms, gesturing for a hug but Smother thinks it's for her so she steps into his arms hugging him tightly saying, "Oh Liam, I was so scared, that cat has problems. I think you should find it a new home, you have your wife and unborn child to consider now, you do not need a wretched cat, especially one that wants to kill everything or worse still, torture things. Imagine if that was your baby!" Liam looks at me over Smother's shoulders to roll his eyes when she pipes up with, "I heard that Liam!"

Before I know it, Smother has already got the rubber gloves on with bleach in hand and is telling me to leave the room like something out of C.I.S. I offer to help but she insists that breathing in too much bleach would harm our little bean so she orders me into the lounge to eat croissants and who can complain at that? I'll tell you who – Liam, walking behind me muttering, "What's she doing here? Why is she so early, I want a cup of coffee if I'm up and I am not even allowed in my own kitchen?"

"Seriously Liam, what's your problem? My mum is in there scrubbing our kitchen, disposing of a dead pigeon and all you can think about is coffee. I'll tell you what, you do it all and I'll call Mum in here for croissants." Taking a deep breath, I devour a whole croissant in one mouthful whilst still managing to give Liam a death stare, I'm not sure he knows what this stare is as he is just looking at me weirdly. I think he is trying to work out if I'm choking or not.

Finally, we make it out of the house and considering what sort of morning we've already had, Smother is surprisingly chipper, singing away in the car as loudly as she can and of course it's the legend that goes by the name of Whitney so we know every word, every pause, every breath. It's just so good to sing out loud, the baby is going mental in my tummy either it is trying to tell me to shut up or it's having the most awesome party in there. I'm hoping the latter as this kid will have to get used to mine and Smother's outbursts of song; my life is like a musical as without any given reason we can just burst into song - its friggin' brilliant!

Walking around the shops looking for baby bits is so much fun; the shops are filled with cute Christmas baby bits, there is Christmas music blaring out of the stores' speakers and there is the smell of mulled wine. It's hard to believe next Christmas I will have my own little elf. Our trolley is full up of useless things this baby won't even need but everything is just so damn cute we have to buy it. For instance, they do these weird squeaky rubber toys now that are for teething that come in the shape of a giraffe which looks like a dog toy. So I bought it because if the baby doesn't use it our dog will (sharing's caring).

Oooooh, another thing to watch out for when pregnant is all the psychic people that seem to come out of the woodwork. I have lost count of how many people just stare at you – well, staring at the belly more like - looking you straight in the eyes and say, "Mmmmm, going by the shape of you I think you're having a boy." Or some people even get you to turn around to examine your derriere to see how much junk you're carrying on your backside and then say, "Oh yes, you're carrying mainly from behind, its definitely a girl, you mark my words. I'm always right at this sort of thing, I've got a bit of witch in me, you know!"

Looks to me there are a lot of witches floating around and they are all saying different things, maybe they need to regroup and have a chat about their psychic abilities. Plus, if there are witches just hanging about and only declaring themselves witches when they see a pregnant woman then that's just weird - are they baby snatchers? If so, I think some witch hunting should commence! It's pretty damn obvious it's going to be a boy or a girl as that is science. I haven't heard yet of a human giving birth to an orangutan or any other species so I'm taking a guess it's safe to say chances are, it's going to be a human baby girl or boy.

CHAPTER ELEVEN

PICKING NAMES

WEDNESDAY 9TH JANUARY 2019

January is definitely the worst month, it's a depressing time of the year as you have just had all the excitement of Christmas shopping, you deal with the short days because you tell yourself it's cosy and it's magical because Christmas is around the corner then BAM! The shit month comes into sight, the short days are now just cold and dark, everyone is skint and did I mention it's cold?

I am now 6 and ½ months pregnant and lying awake again, staring up at the ceiling and pondering whether to smother my husband whilst he sleeps because of his incessant snoring – it's driving me FUCKING mad but the nice side of me tells me that it wouldn't be the best idea. I mean, when he is awake you do actually love him, it's just when he's asleep that he gets right up your nose. Keep remembering all the good things he does for you: he loves you dearly, he's a wizard at putting stuff together, plus we have previously established we really don't want to give birth in prison do we? I take another look over to him sleeping, still snoring like Shrek, and again he is beginning to piss me off so I decide to get up. Good move Soph, I'm proud of you for not reacting and for letting him sleep peacefully, well for now anyway. I make my way downstairs to have a hot chocolate with whipped cream and marshmallows. I thought if I'm up I better make myself happy about being up and guess what? Cream and mallows does that . . . oh and a twirl.

Sitting in front of the telly, flicking through to see what's on and wow, it's crap at this time in the early hours. So I decide to look for a name for our bundle of joy. Who knew there were so many names? And weird names too! Here are a few I found: Bran, Coyote, Sugar, Cub, Lark, Jungle, Zeplin, Kaptain . . . I don't want to offend anyone but if any of those take your fancy it's just NO, NO, NO! Do not call your child Jungle or any of those names above, just no. So now I have told you what you can't call your baby, now let me tell you the ones I do like. Oh and don't be knob heads and start disliking my names just because Jungle is the shittiest name on planet Earth.

Now that's clear, here are a few:

1. Pearl 2. Libby 3. Sophia 4. Amelia 5. Harper

1. Axel 2. Jackson 3. Zachary 4. Oh I can't look anymore, I'm bored.

Snuggled up on the sofa feeling sleepy again, I try and close my eyes and relax but all I can hear is the dog licking his balls. Grrrrr, if it isn't Shrek upstairs, it's the bloody dog downstairs - all I need is Psycho Cat to make an appearance and that will be a full house of twats.

Liam wakes up at 7am to go to work, he is trotting down the stairs like a gazelle full of happiness with a real spring in his step. I'm not surprised with a solid 8 hours kip under his belt. I am telling myself, DO NOT BE A BITCH, DO NOT MAKE SNARKY COMMENTS, DO NOT GIVE HIM THE COLD SHOULDER. Well, two out of three ain't bad eh???

In the salon, I am subdued. People are noticing I am not myself but I can see and feel they are scared to say anything to me; to be honest so they should be. I am slowly realising I'm not so happy-go-lucky anymore about this whole pregnancy malarkey. I am getting fatter quicker than someone can say crispy spring roll, oh why did I have to mention food? Now I'm hungry and my patience for people's shit is really wearing me down. I will give you an example: a client sits in the chair and we have a chat about what they want. Now these are her words, not mine:

"I would like highlights, natural highlights. I don't want any sort of yellow though and I don't like ash. I want them a creamy colour so it looks all year round sun-kissed like I'm a natural blonde."

Now her hair is a base 4 - to all of you that don't know this talk, that's dark; really, really dark. She also has a box colour on her head and has a regrowth of 3 inches. I can tell you all now that it isn't going creamy in one sitting. Trying to explain this to her though is like I'm speaking in Korean. Her face looked so confused: "But I've seen it on Instagram, they all have dark hair and turn out really blonde?"

"Well, if you want to stay here for 8 hours and let me bleach it over and over until your hair can't take anymore then you can give me £400 for the pleasure of you having haystack frazzled hair. Yes, I can give you creamy highlights which will look like you have lived by yourself on a desert island for 8 years so I suppose it will look natural cave-woman like. The decision is yours my lovely."

The client opted to take my professional opinion and go with what I know! I hope I wasn't too hard on her but sometimes you just need to be told and not fanny-arse around with these things. You all want Insta hair or Pinterest hair which sometimes lie to you: it isn't always what the eye sees.

Rant over. Client's hair looked gorgeous, she was over the moon and no one died so good day all round I say.

Paul pops into the salon looking flustered and asking if I have seen Amy, his otherhalf, "No, sorry Paul, why, have you lost her?"

"Ha ha, no, not as such, she just has my phone and I thought I overheard a conversation saying she was due to have her hair done."

"No sorry, not with me she isn't." I look through the appointment bookings to see if she was in anywhere but can't see her. Looking up at Paul, he looks as if he is about to cry. "Don't worry, I'm sure she has your phone safe, is it that you need to call someone? You can use mine, phone her and see where she is."

"That's a great idea, thanks Soph." Snatching the phone out of my hand, slamming it to his ear, pacing up and down the salon looking very worried, he takes the phone away from his ear to redial again. Obviously no answer, he slowly hands me the phone back.

"Paul, are you ok?" He looks sweaty and pale.

"Yeah I'm ok, don't worry Soph, I'll probably be round yours later if that's ok?"

"Of course it is, you know you don't need an invite, you're basically family Luv. Whatever it is, it will be ok I'm sure."

"Yeah, you're right, see ya later on." Within a blink of an eye he was gone. The girls are peering like meerkats through the back-room door trying to listen and peek at what's just happened.

I have asked my clients to write down names they might like for this baby, to give me inspiration, as to be honest, all the joy has been sucked out of me today. I have ten bits of paper to look at later whilst eating doughnuts and drinking hot choc with whipped cream on top, yum yum. Oooh look, a slither of joy has returned. On my way home I pop in to see

Mum and dad, thank the lord they haven't got music blaring out this time, and sit down at the kitchen table whilst Dad makes me a hot chocolate. His words are, "Anything for my little girl." As I sit there feeling special, I notice a magazine open on the table to a page which looks like a picture of Sweden with scribbles of writing all over it: dates and times.

"You going somewhere, dad?"

"Yeah maybe, your mum and I are only thinking about it"

"Oooh looks fancy"

"Yes but as I say we are only thinking about it as it would be for a while"

"what do you mean a while?"

"Maybe a year"

"A YEAR WHY?"

"Well your Mum has always wanted to go and we both are retirement age and healthy so we thought why not travel and see parts of the world that we have always wanted to see"

"WHY CANT YOU BOTH BE NORMAL, RETIRE. SIT DO NOTHING, GO FOR A WALK EVERY NOW AND THEN"

"Why you shouting?"

"WHOS SHOUTING NO ONE IS SHOUTING"

"Oh Soph what is really wrong?"

"I am having a baby and I am scared that's what is wrong I don't know the first thing about having a baby, you guys have been there done it, I am living proof you both done an okish job. I need help"

"Myself and your Mum will always be there for you don't worry darling, anyway your going to be a fabulous mum you wont need any help"

Feeling fragile and scared my eyes begin to well up, Dad sees this and pulls me close and reassures me not to worry and that they both will always be there for me and the baby. I feel sad and selfish all at the same time, they both have worked hard all their adult lives who am I to stop them from living the lives they deserve. "Dad its ok I want you and Mum to go have fun" "Shhhhh lets not talk about it now darling just relax and enjoy your hot choccy."

CHAPTER TWELVE

ANTENATAL CLASSES

WEDNESDAY 6TH FEBUARY 2019

Waking from tormented sleep to soon figure out that I am going to be tormented awake too. What the hell is all the noise about downstairs? I can hear two voices, male ones; one voice sounds agitated, the other, calmer, but I can tell they are getting annoyed. What is even the time? I glance over to the clock: 6AM! WTAF? I'm gonna go apeshit as soon as I've waddled to the toilet to empty my camel's bladder as nowadays I think this baby is using my bladder as a trampoline.

I waddle to the top of the stairs to try and listen to the voices downstairs. I can hear Liam telling the other voice to shut up, then the other voice is sounding upset. I walk down the stairs trying to be quiet as a mouse but who am I kidding, right now I'm more like a fairy elephant pounding its way down the stairs, each step feeling like its bending with my weight these days.

I reach the front room when the voices suddenly stop talking. I slowly open the door to find Paul and Liam looking at me like a rabbit caught in headlights, standing still very still as if staying still and quiet I might not see them. Well lads, this isn't Jurassic park I REALISE that I am the width of a dinosaur but believe it or not, I'M NOT ACTUALLY ONE!

"Hi Paul, how are you?"

"Yeah I'm good Soph, you?"

"Funny you should ask that, do you know what time it is?"

"Yes so sorry, I've had a bit a row with Amy."

"Oh I'm sorry to hear this, is she ok?"

"Is she ok? What about me? It isn't my fault."

"Ok, sorry I asked." Liam walks over to me to hug me. I snuggle into his chest and look at Paul with angry eyes who looks back at me with even angrier eyes. I pull away and head out to the kitchen to make breakfast. Liam is walking behind me apologising for all the noise when I turn to look at him whilst yelling over his shoulder to Paul, "Do you want a cup of tea and toast seeing as you're here?"

"Yes please, can I have jam on my toast thanks?" I look at Liam with a look that he knows only too well, replying with, "Breathe, just breathe and count to ten slowly, anger isn't good for the baby. I shoot him a look as he scuttles off out of the kitchen, telling him to get Paul out of our house as we have antenatal classes to get ready for. The excitement in his sigh is overwhelming.

Mark phones me on the way to the class to tell me the venue has changed due to an overbooking of the room; apparently a Catholic service is more important than knowing how to get a small human out of something the size of a 1p coin. On the way to the new venue, I quiz Liam about Paul, "Why was he at our house so early then, must have been a big bust up for him to turn up that early?"

"Oh Soph, you know what Paul and Amy are like, he probably forgot to put the bins out or something stupid like that."

"He was telling you though what it was when I came down?"

"I'm going to tell you something now Soph that may shock you . . . I don't always listen. I may look like I'm listening but in actual fact I'm thinking about food."

"NO SHIT SHERLOCK! You actually think I don't already know this but this is your best mate, you need to listen to him, he could be in a bad place right now and all you're doing is day-dreaming about pancakes."

We pull up at the new venue which is very apt for this class as it's in the labour ward – well, I say in the labour ward, it's actually a small room just off of the labour ward. Liam walks into the room first with myself following closely behind. I say closely, my stomach is so big now that even if my stomach is touching Liam's back, the rest of my body is trailing 10ft behind . . . it feels like that anyway. As I walk in the room I catch Mark's eye, he winks at me and tells me that it's going to be a fun morning. I respond with a simple smile. In the class there are five couples, we all seem a little nervous as I'm assuming we are all first time mothers because surely if you have already had a baby why oh why would you come to this class again unless you want to relive the horror story of what's about to happen to you again in the next few coming weeks. We all get asked to take a seat by what I can only describe as the most beautiful woman I ever have ever seen; her hair is long, dark and effortlessly half up, half down almost like she has got hot and just scraped half back in a claw clip. The hair that it hanging down her back is bouncy, swinging from side to side as she moves and her skin is pure, no blemishes and hardly any make-up. She is dressed in smart, Paperbag waist trousers with a tee shirt tucked in and she obviously works out as her firm buttocks look as if they could crack a walnut in half. As I gaze at her beauty I find myself feeling angry and I'm not sure why . . . oh yes, I jeffing do, who the f**k thought it funny to put this goddess in front of a bunch of heavily pregnant, hormonal, first time mothers? This woman is going to get eaten alive. If I am having these thoughts of how bloody perfect she is, imagine all the men? These men have had to cope with watching our bodies change almost daily, cope with our ever-changing mood swings and have to deal with the word NO a lot. I can see in these women's eyes that we feel like shit about our bodies. Don't get me wrong, I love my body because I am creating life but having the map of the world from your veins and stretch marks on your ever-growing belly can wear a little thin especially when you have the spitting image of Megan Fox standing in front of you. I wonder how many of these couples have an argument after they leave here, how many of the women accuse their blokes for checking out Miss Fitty because let's be honest, we all have. Poor female, she's in for a tough ride with this lot.

Mark stands up to introduce himself and to give us a quick run through of why we are all here then Fitty gets up do the same. "Hi everyone my name is Bella." HOLD UP, ARE YOU CLUCKING KIDDING ME RIGHT NOW? EVEN HER NAME ACTUALLY MEANS BEAUTIFUL IN ITALIAN. WHERE'S MY COAT, I'M LEAVING!

"I am here along with Mark to show you what the most effective way of dealing with the pain of child birth is."... Ok I'd better stay, I need to know this vital information, I'll let Beautiful continue. Mark walks round the room offering drinks and biscuits to us; everyone in the room takes a drink but only the men take the snacks as all the women are already on a diet just from being in the room with Miss Beautiful for ten minutes. Miss beautiful begins the story of the first signs of labour:

"1. You may have some bouts of diarrhoea as the muscles in your rectum relax, it's the body's natural way of having a final clear out before the big event.

2. You can lose your mucus plug, this is a thick snot like consistency cork effect that has been keeping all the germs away from your baby. Once this comes out you may think that labour is about to introduce itself. Maybe for some it's imminent or maybe not, you can lose your plug one to two weeks before labour, but the good sign is it's definitely going in the right direction."

Liam made a noise at the words 'mucus plug' and I look around the room to find most of the men squinting and pulling a face of disgust. One couple however are super intense with each other; the husband is sitting next to his love with a note pad and pen stroking her leg while she has the biggest smile on her face . . . in fact, she almost looks high.

"3. Your waters may break. This is not always the case, sometimes we need to help with this part of labour. I'm sure all the ladies in the room know what this is but a recap for you doesn't hurt and for the guys in the room it's important you know what's happening, so you don't panic. Your waters are called the amniotic sac, it's a bag of fluid that surrounds your baby in the womb. When the sac breaks, the water comes out - now this can happen suddenly like a fast gush of water but it's more likely to start as a trickle like you've left a tap dripping. So guys, if the gush does happen, stay calm. You won't need to build an ark as it's over in a split second, just make your loved ones feel calm and secure."

Mark is smiling at me gesturing for me to look at Liam. I turn my head and I think it's already too much for him for I can see the cogs of his brain whirling away. I snigger and look back at Mark to make a silly face.

"4. Contractions may start, this is a tightening of the tummy in early stage of labour these will begin short and far apart. Don't think just because you are getting contractions you need to come up to the hospital as your contractions could just disappear for a while. You don't want to come up here for us to assess you only to find your only 2cm dilated for us to then send you back home. My advice is to stay at home for as long as possible, have a nice warm bath put some music on enjoy each other's company as two will soon become 3 or 4 depending on how many babies you're carrying."

She looks at me when she says that, cheeky cow, thinking I have two in here. Newsflash lady, it's only one. Her beauty is diminishing by the minute.

"5. When your contractions become stronger and closer together it's time to join us lovely lot up here on Labour Suite. We will examine you to see how far along you are, this is where we insert two fingers either side of the cervix opening and estimate how far apart they are. Hopefully you will all be around 3-4cm. This is called active stage of labour, we will then check you every hour as it's expected to open quicker in this stage."

Mark stands up to hand out some playdough to everyone and I start making things with mine. I start with the classic snake then I move onto a bear with cute little ears and a nose. Whilst I am making my little animals, I overhear Mark say, "Right, I am going to come round and see how dilated you are with the playdough that I gave you."

What shit, I wasn't listening - what does he mean dilated, what were we supposed to be doing? I hear him say to the couple next to me, "That's great, you are 6cm dilated." He has his two fingers either side of the ring mould that the couple have made. He then turns to me, "So Soph, let's see how dilated you are?" I look up at him, shaking my head - no no no - but he continues to proceed: "Come on Soph, hand over your Cervix." I hand over a playdough pig - a very good playdough pig I'll have you all know. Mark looks at me silently for a second but then begins to laugh. No one knows yet why he is laughing, then of course he holds piggy up high above his head and says "I am not qualified to examine how far pigs are dilated." Everybody chuckles, well everyone except Liam who doesn't see the funny side, just looking at the floor. Mark hands me back my pig and thanks me for brightening up his day.

"6. In the active stage of labour you start to feel tired, irritable which a warning for you lads. Keep your loved one calm, try to listen to what she needs and don't get annoyed with her if she shouts at you, as this stage is very tiring."

"7. Transition Phase: this in my experience is the most challenging as the contractions are very close together but even though it's the most challenging it's also the shortest stage, your cervix at this stage is able to dilate fully. Contractions should last 60-90 seconds with a rest of two minutes in-between. In this stage you may feel hot, sick or gassy. Gents, avoid small talk at this stage, believe me, she won't thank you for talking about the weather instead of giving her encouragement, Hold her hand, try to encourage sips of water."

I look at Liam and he is still looking at the floor, "Are you ok babe?"

"Yeah why?"

"Only you have been counting the floor tiles for ten minutes."

"Yeah I'm fine, just a lot to take in, isn't it?"

"Yeah it is but it will be ok, I love you." Liam looks at me intensely with what looks like a tear in his eye. "I love you too Soph." Mark is over the other side of the room rummaging through a bag. He has two objects in his hands and I can't figure out what they are. Bella is still chatting about the phases of labour.

"8. Second stage of labour." How many stages are there? Holy Mackerel, I know I have been there for Louise but it all seem a blur now, I don't remember any midwife shouting out second stage! "The Second stage is where the baby's making its way down the birth canal ready to make its way into this world. In this stage you will experience intense pressure almost like you need a big poo." A big POO? Wow, if you're pooing that out, you have issues. "With each contraction, your midwife will encourage you to push." Mark for some reason has put on a swimming hat, maybe it's nearly over and is planning on going swimming. Bella turns to Mark with a smile . . . why is she so bloody beautiful? Her smile could melt the heart of an ice queen. Mark is smiling back with his perfect smile also. "Mark is going to demonstrate how a baby comes out of the vagina." One bloke laughs which then has a knock on effect to the rest of the group as now Mark is slowly putting on a roll neck. His arms are in but his head is yet to appear. Oh I get it, that's why he has a swimming hat on. Bella is pretending to have a contraction, doing her breathing exercises and asking us all to join in. So now in this room you have a bunch of people breathing to the point of passing out and some guy with a swimming cap on slowly, slowly emerging through the neck of a roll neck with each pretend contraction and Fitty giving a running commentary on how far Cap Head is out of the roll neck, showing us what crowning would look like. I bloody hope not as the swimming cap is bright green and the roll neck is mustard yellow! I can't help but laugh and glance at Liam to see the first smile on his face since we have arrived here, so maybe something good has come out of this day trip, Liam's facial muscles are actually working.

The green-headed baby has been born out of the roll neck. All is well - it's a healthy 30 year-old man with designer stubble and a full set of gleaming white teeth. Bella continues to tell us about the afterbirth, as you remember I thought it just got dragged out but I'm so pleased she is telling the rest this bit of vital info.

Nearing the end of the class now which I am happy about as I'm STARVING MARVIN, I think I could eat a small Shetland. Bella thanks us all for being so wonderful and lovely. Wow, not only is she beautiful, she is also lovely; bloody annoying there is nothing to hate about this girl. Quick let's make an exit before I turn fully fledged lesbo. Mark walks over to us as Liam scuttles off to the car before giving Mark a chance to say goodbye. It does make me chuckle how Liam feels slightly awkward with Mark, I don't make any comment about it as Liam would just act even worse if known to the fact I see what I see. Mark gives me a squeeze and asks me how I thought it was. "It was great, sorry if I zoned out for the dilation bit." Mark laughs, "Don't apologise, that made my day, you look beautiful today by the way, you look radiant."

"Yes, radiant with sweat don't you mean?"

"Just take a compliment Soph, please. Was Liam ok today, he looked a bit distracted?"

"I think so, to be honest I think realisation has hit home today that we are having a baby very soon. I just think he is worried, he will be ok."

"Good, glad to hear it, I want you to be as calm as possible having this baby, you know where I am if you need me. You have my number, just text me any time, day or night."

"Thank you Mark, you know just the right things to say to keep us mummies calm."

CHAPTER THIRTEEN

BABY SHOWER

FRIDAY 1ST MARCH 2019

In the salon I am feeling bigger by the hour but everyone is just so lovely telling me how lovely and glowing I look which is beginning to piss me off! I know I should be loving all the attention but I just don't. I mean, I don't actually have to work anymore but what would I do if I was at home and even though the littlest of thing are grating on me I do actually love being at work. I love the chit chat, the giggles and the gossip of the girls' vibrant lives. I will give up two weeks before so I only have another 3 weeks of hair and gossip anyway.

Louise sticks her head in the door with kids in tow to ask me if I had a gap for a cuppa. I tell her I'll be five minutes and will meet her down the road in this new café I have been wanting to check it out anyway.

I grab my coat, pop it on and go to do up the zip only to remember I'm too fat for it to do up. I just look down at my tummy and tell myself I can eat another cake as it's not doing up anyway. I tap my belly and giggle. You must laugh at these things.

Ooooh, it's nice in this café, very modern but Louise is glaring at me from the other side so I walk over to her and sit down. "What's up?"

"Have you seen the menu in here?"

"No why?"

"Let's just say if you're a fan of grains and seeds then we will be ok. I don't think this is a normal café." Felix is not convinced with a bowl of . . . erm, I'm not even sure what that bowl of stuff is. He picks up his spoon and digs straight in. The face he pulls first is looking good but then it quickly changes into what looks like a bush tucker trial face, opening his mouth wide, sticking out his tongue and wiping it with a napkin. I think the verdict is a no then. Felix quickly goes into Louise's bag for his survival stash of chocolate buttons. Louise and I chew on some very grainy, nutty bread with a couple of bowls of raw veg then have the pleasure of paying the earth for it . . . funny that that's where most of it came out from.

Louise is looking fabulous; her hair is clean, she is in actual clothes and she loves all things life can bring today. "You're happy today, why?"

"What do you mean? I'm always happy."

"Just you saying that is weird, are you on medication?" Louise laughs a really high pitched laugh, the laugh only hyenas can hear. "You're being weird and it's freaking me out!" More laughing follows and when she finally stops that weird noise coming out from her mouth, she says, "I hope you're free next Sunday, we are doing something. Oh and look pretty, get a new dress or something."

"A new dress, are you kidding? Dresses don't fit me anymore, I have taken up shopping in Mountain Warehouse these days as the only things that fit me are tents!" Louise looks at me in a sympathetic way and says, "Shut the f**k up and stop feeling sorry for yourself, wait for pregnancy number two then you can complain of what a sack of s**t you look like but until then go and buy yourself something nice and get on with it."

"Welcome back babe, not sure who took over your body but it was weird."

"Oh shut up."

We left the café laughing, I was pushing the pushchair for Louise whilst she ran up the road trying to catch Felix, yelling at him to stop when he gets to the road. Of course, it doesn't look like he is listening so Louise is getting increasingly louder as she runs faster to scoop Felix up into a rugby lift under one arm. He is laughing so hard under her arm I think he has wet himself. Louise however is a shade of purple and is breathing like she has just run a marathon. She comes into the salon with me to see Smother and of course, Smother gets Hugo out of his pram for snuggles, making comments like, "Oooohhhh I can't wait till this one makes an appearance so I can have snuggles." She takes in a big long breath of the top of Hugo's head almost as if she was sucking some of the youth out of his small body, "Mum, please stop smelling him!"

"Oh but Soph, he smells so good!"

"Really mum? You like the smell of sick and poo then?"

"No Soph, he smells like a baby still, even though he is getting so big, so quick. I can't believe he is nearly seven months old." Louise isn't even in reception anymore but from the back of the salon she notices Felix has the Velcro curler tray out and is sticking them to Mrs Brackley's head, who is bending down encouraging his behaviour telling Louise how adorable he is. Louise responds affirming it's fine when the things he is sticking to your head are soft and squidgy rather than a swift swipe of a remote control at your temple.

Louise grabs Felix and asks Smother to put Hugo in his pram as we only have a two minute window before laughing turns to screams from Felix. Be quick ladies - quicker than that - someone get the door and within a blink of an eye, Louise is gone. Watching her walk up the road with Felix under one arm whilst pushing a pram with the other, I realise this woman is still my hero. She may not be graceful but she is Wonder Woman and Harley Quinn all wrapped into one.

As I arrive home, I notice Paul's car outside the house, entering the hallway and see bags on the floor. "Hey you guys, where are you?"

"We are in the kitchen babe." Walking through the kitchen door, I smell food, home-cooked food which smells delicious, "Mmmmmm what's that smell?" Paul walks over to me, takes my hand and guides me over to the kitchen table, pushing me onto the seat. Liam then walks over with a cup of tea for me. "What's all this?"

"We thought we would cook for you as I know how tired you are getting now." Paul is getting closer with spag bol in his hands, "Yummy thanks guys."

"I'm sorry for waking you up the other morning, Soph."

"Oh all is forgiven Paul, especially if there is food involved." As I inhale the food looking nowhere else but at my plate I can feel an uneasy vibe in the room. "Why can I feel you staring at me boys?" "It's a hell of a sight to see someone inhale food that quickly!" Liam punches Paul in the arm and tells him to shut up and comes and sits next to me, stroking my arm. "Soph, I have something to ask you."

"Ok what is it?"

"Well, Paul has split up with Amy and he has nowhere to stay, can he crash here for a while?" Paul is looking at me with big puppy eyes. "We are close to having a baby Liam."

"I know but Paul can help out like cook and clean. I think it will actually be good for us, take some of the stress off us." I sat and pondered for a second whilst licking my plate, "Ok fine but you better have more dishes up your sleeve." Paul walks over to me and kisses me fully on the lips. "Thank you Soph, I cannot tell you what this means to me."

Sunday 10th March 2019

A week later and everyone is being weirder than usual. Liam's really happy, Paul is always singing and can't do enough for me so I think I actually like living with two men. I had my doubts as I had visions of the boys getting drunk every night, acting like idiots, but it's the total opposite. It's very calm and we all have a giggle. Paul has taken it upon himself to be head chef, Liam is getting jobs done around the house and garden, I have top-ups of tea and juice and I feel like a celeb. This is what Beyoncé must feel like.

One thing that is doing my head in is Louise not taking my calls and Smother is making lame excuses not to see me. My tummy keeps tightening today, no pain which tells me things are getting really close. "I'm going to go see Nan," I yell as I walk out, I'll be back soon. I get in the car and just about to shut the door when Liam falls out of it yelling at me. "No Soph, you can't go anywhere!"

"Eh yes I can, watch this."

"Soph NO. Please can you just get out of the car?"

What the jeffin hell is wrong with people today, why is he being a weirdo? "What's wrong with you Liam, why are you acting like a paranoid freak? Telling me I can't go see my nan who is an old lady and may only have 10 minutes left on this planet!"

Ok, quick update: my nan is some sort of supernatural freak and will outlive all of us. She's frickin' amazeballs and even though Liam knows this, it doesn't hurt to make him feel a little guilty about me going to see her.

"Sophie, just get out of the car and get in my van."

"Get in your van! You're sounding like a typical kidnapper

now, I mean not that I know what a typical kidnapper sounds like but they say it on the films so with that evidence, you are!" Paul is now at the door acting like a twat pretending to be a bouncer, what a knob!

"Fine but just so you know, I don't want to."

Liam drives us to a pub car park and tells me to get out. I'm still moody so I ignore his request but he just walks round to my side and opens the door for me. I look down at him from my seat as he holds his hand out to me to help me down which of course, I refuse and leap like a gazelle out of the chair. Realising quickly the size of me and the weight, guess what? The floor comes up a lot sooner than I plan it in my head and as the ground finally stops shaking from my leap, I can feel something wet on my leg. Oh great, I've only gone and wet myself, as if today couldn't get any better. Luckily I have spare knickers . . . remember girls always pack spare knickers!

"I need to get back in the van Liam, I've wet myself!"

"You've what?"

"Erm, what part of wet myself didn't you understand?"

"How?"

"Liam, this isn't a conversation I want to have right now, just let me change my knickers."

"Where?"

"IN THE VAN." I lift one leg up to the step and there it was - WOOSH a warm feeling down my leg on the car park floor. "Soph I hate to say this but you're still weeing, Jesus that's a lot of piss!"

"Liam I'm not sure that's wee."

"What is it then?"

"I think it's the baby"

"I expected it to be more solid than that! Oh shit, has it gone under the van?"

"LIAM NO, IT HASN'T GONE UNDER THE VAN, I THINK MY WATERS HAVE BROKEN!"

"OH MY GOD! OK DON'T PANIC! I'm going to go get help." Liam has run off into the pub, great, that's all I need: a load of piss heads trying to help me. I look down at the floor and see I'm still dripping, it's like a tap that just won't shut off. Maybe if I shove my dress in-between my legs and squish my legs together that might help. Nope, that's done nothing. I can't have the baby now, it's early by about four weeks. I still have clients in for the next two weeks; who's going to do their hair? Oh my days, who's going to do MY hair? I had planned a pamper day when I went on maternity leave, I need some high-lights and a conditioning treatment plus a trim. Oh great, now I'm crying, why are you crying? It's not supposed to be here yet, I'm not ready, why not? Because I need my hair done and what if the baby is not ok? Listen to yourself Soph, babies come early all the time, you look amazing, you're going to make the best mum in the world, our baby wants to meet us and who can blame it? We are great! You're right, we are, we're funny, loving and funny. You've said that one. I know but it's good to be funny. Ok let's do this. Thanks Wiser Me, we really can do this, I just may need your help a bit more than usual in the next few weeks. No problem, I'm always here, you know that.

I look up from the ground to see Louise, Mark, Smother and Liam running towards me, behind them, the work family and Nan. Mark is first to my side which I am glad about as he is the professional. I don't need anyone else's advice right now, but guess what, they are going to give it anyway. Hang on, why is everyone at the pub? "Hi Mark, sorry to drag you out of the pub, I'll go and apologise to your partner in a minute, I just need to dry off a bit before I do."

"My partner isn't here, she's probably on a date with her new guy."

"What? She . . ."

"Yeah, she left me."

"What, you're not . . ."

"Not together anymore, No."

"What is going on? I don't quite understand what's happening."

"Well, your waters have broken which means you're in labour. Have you been feeling any contractions?"

"No, I get that I'm in labour, I don't get why my people are here, what's happening Mark?"

"It's supposed to be your baby shower this afternoon but I think your baby has other plans."

"Baby shower????"

Everyone now has circled me like a pack of wolves, laughing and telling me how exciting this is and offering me their advice. I tell you what they haven't offered me yet, a chair! Mark has gone to go get his car as he thinks Liam's van is too high for me to climb back into. Liam looks a shade of grey and as he is walking around the car park on his phone, he keeps glancing over to me doing a weird nodding thing. Mark pulls up and Smother helps me to the side of the car, I try to tell her I'm fine but no, she insists on running back into the pub to grab a plastic tablecloth for me to sit on. Mark has got a fancy car, I don't think he wants whatever liquid you have leaking from you all over it. Sitting in the car looking out onto my family waving at me, giggling their little heads off, I am actually feeling very emotional. They are all weirdos in their own little ways but they are my weirdos whom I love enormously, I feel very lucky to have all these people in my life that care for me. As Mark pulls away I can see Smother crying into the arms of Nan who is doing a good job of comforting her by stroking her hair. I suppose it's true what they say: once a mum, always a mum.

Driving to the hospital was fun it was like I was sitting on a wet piece of tarpaulin, every time we went around a corner I slid off it, I would go as far to say it was like having a go on a really shit waterslide. Mark was being his amazing self by keeping calm asking me if I was having any contractions or discomfort, which I wasn't, weird right?

"Why are we going to the hospital Mark? Why can't I just go home?"

"It's because your waters have broken, we like to check you over or have you in due to infection risk because your waters have gone."

"I could be in for ages though as I feel fine."

"No you won't be in too long as they don't like to leave you that long if your waters have gone, we will speed things up for you by putting you on a drip to start your contractions. I must say Soph, you'll be the most beautiful mum-to-be in the ward; luckily you're a hairdresser as your hair always looks good."

"Thank you Mark, that's really sweet of you. Erm . . . why have you split up with your partner actually? I'm sorry, I don't mean to pry."

"No, it's fine, she just found someone else. I can't really blame her, he's much better looking than me; roughly 6ft 4 and a much wider chest span than mine. Hey ho, you win some, you lose some. Oh and I think he's in the building trade so I am guessing she likes someone with a more MANLY job? Who knows? Anyway stop talking about me, you're the one in labour here, it's your day."

"Well I think she is total poo-head, she doesn't know a good thing even if it slapped her in the face. She'll be sorry and come crawling back with her tail between her legs, mark my words." Ha ha ha – Mark! Ha ha ha, see what I did there? I NEED HELP.

CHAPTER FOURTEEN

LABOUR

Arriving at the hospital I notice Liam waiting at the entrance pacing up and down like a caged animal, a look of worry on his face. I look at Mark and all of a sudden, I start to panic.

"Why did I think I can do this? I have a smear test and pass out Mark, why do I think I can push a baby out of me and be ok?"

"Soph you're going to be absolutely fine, Liam is here, I am here but truth be told, don't think you need anyone, you are going to be amazing."

Liam appears at the door of the car smiling his fake smile he does when he is trying to cover up his real feelings.

On the ward it's very busy: people rushing around like a headless chickens, some midwives are smiling in the chaos and some are scowling and doing a lot of huffing. I get taken to a room and told to make myself comfortable . . . are they joking? Look at me, I'm damp from the waist down and I look like I have swallowed an exercise ball, how do they expect me to get comfy? I know not the right attitude I should have right now as I know this is the beginning to a very horrible middle but hopefully a nice ending.

Liam has sanitised his hands 6 times now, he won't have any skin left at this rate. His phone rings and I see it's Paul. "Hi mate I can't talk right now, Soph is in labour I think, well I mean her waters burst all over the pub carpark and I'm told that's labour. Yeah, yeah, I will call you in a bit, yeah yeah, you too mate, see ya." Liam looks at me trying to swing my legs up on the bed without falling backwards like a beetle stuck on its back. I am huffing and puffing as gravity takes over and pulls me backwards onto the pillow so now I am trying to sit up. Bloody hell this is hard work. Mark appears through the door in uniform with a huge grin on his face. Liam at this point takes a step closer to me, looking uncomfortable - a bit like me really.

Mark stands at the end of the bed with a clip board and a pen then walks round the bed to lift my arm to attach a blood pressure machine to it and still grinning like a Cheshire cat. "What's happened to your face Mark, why are you smiling so much and should you even be here?"

"I am smiling because I'm excited you're having a baby and no, I shouldn't be here but I really want to deliver your baby if that's ok with you?" Now in my head, I'm saying I was ok with it when I thought he was gay but now I will have two straight men looking at my foo foo and I am not sure how I feel about that, I mean I wouldn't batter an eye lid at a male doctor so I suppose this is no different but why does it feel slightly weird. "I really want to thank you Soph for being just so lovely through all of this, not once have you made me feel uncomfortable about being a midwife. Some people question it but not you, thank you." Oh crap, how can I send him away now? "Oh Mark, no thanks needed, no one should ever be so narrow-minded, you're a brilliant midwife." Quickly recovered brain, well done!

Laying on the bed in a hospital gown now and Liam is still pacing up and down next to the window, Mark however is now at the business end of things about to examine me. He tells me to relax and then proceeds to do his job of seeing how dilated I am. Liam is now at my side breathing as if he has someone shoving their hand up his arse looking at me wide eyed, not blinking. This look I have seen before with Louise's birth: it's the look of fear and realisation that shit's about to get real very quickly. "Calm down Liam, it's going to be ok, I am the one having to go through the pain and at the end we will have a beautiful baby. Try not to panic and if you find it too much at any point, just head out for some air ok?" With that Liam just nods at me and walks out of the room . . . wow, he didn't need much convincing did he?

Mark drags out his hand from the abyss and tells me I am already four and a half centimetres dilated which is great because I have had no pain so far.

"Mark, why have I had no pain yet?"

"Don't get used to that, you definitely will. I don't think it will be too long, I am going to go and get gas and air ready for when and if you need it."

He walks out of the room so now I am alone in a room looking at my bump when I suddenly feel what I think is a contraction. It isn't pleasant but it's ok. My stomach went rock hard and felt as if someone was squeezing my rib cage. It only lasted a few seconds and it's all back to normal now. Mark returns with the precious gas and air.

"You're like Yoda, Mark. I just had a contraction, it was fine though, not too bad"

"That's great news, it means everything is going in the right direction. I'll just put this next to you, you won't need it yet though so don't be tempted; only have it when things get really tough. Is Liam ok? I just saw him pacing on the phone outside, he looks grey with fear."

"I told him to get some air and if things get too tough for him he can go outside whenever he feels like it."

"Do you want me to go and have a word, make sure he's ok?"

"That would be great, thank you Mark."

Alone again is when I start to think what my baby is going to look like. Is it going to have hair and if so, what colour will it be? Is it going to have all of its fingers and toes? I hope it hasn't got too big a head as that's the bit that hurts the most. I want it to have a small head but not a pea head. I think a six-pound baby will be fine, I hope you're listening in there. A different midwife pops her head round the door to check if I am ok and to see if I want anything like a cup of tea or some water. Am I allowed wine or gin yet? She laughs, "I'll bring you a cup of tea."

Liam and Mark are back just in time as my contractions are definitely there now. Mark tells me to breathe through each one, as apparently I am holding my breath, but it's starting to hurt now. Liam is holding my hand giving me encouragement. Whatever Mark has said to him has seemed to have worked, he seems a lot more with it. Tea is here, yay, tea will make it better! Tea as I say makes most things better in life. I'm going to try to stand up and have a little wander around the room with my tea. Oh SHIT SHIT SHIT, a huge contraction is taking hold. I drop my tea on the floor clinging onto Mark's arm, I am head down breathin deeply thinking of all the nice things I am grateful for -tea is one of them and its now all over the floor. "I am so sorry, I have made a mess, get me a cloth and I'll clear it up." I am still holding onto Mark tightly who is looking at his upside-down watch on his uniform. He smiles at me and tells me to relax, there probably will be more mess on the floor soon when tea is the last thing to worry about. Finally, it passes and I stand up straight Liam is looking at my phone vibrating on the side table. "It's your dad, do you want me to answer it?"

"Yes please" Another contraction is coming, I can feel it building and taking hold like a boa constrictor on its prey. I have clamped my hands round the bar at the end of the bed and looking at my feet thinking how ugly feet are. Look at them, they are like a cavewoman's feet: veiny, fat, swollen chipolatas as toes. How do some people have feet fetishes? It's gross, bet if they saw my feet right now they would change their fetish pretty quickly, it's enough to make you throw up in your mouth.

"Soph, Soph are you ok down there?" I look up at Liam. "What?"

"I have asked you three times if you are ok and you didn't answer me, you just grunted a weird sound."

"Oh sorry, I didn't answer you because if you haven't noticed, a human is trying to exit my body right now and I was thinking about how ugly my feet are." Mark drags over the gas and air and tells me with the next contraction to try it.

CHAPTER FIFTEEN

IT'S ALL TOO MUCH

STILL SUNDAY . . .

A few hours have gone past, I'm tired but gas and air is great. I feel like I'm on a night out, where are the tunes? Hold that thought, another bloody contraction is here . . . grrrrrrrrrr, Ow! I now have a heart monitor attached to me to check the baby's heart rate and to monitor contractions. It's like wearing a massive black belt with a round thing that sits at the front of my belly and it's uncomfortable, especially when contractions are here.

Mark's face is looking slightly more stressed than it did earlier when he pops out of the room. I look at Liam who is also looking pale. Mark come back with other people who look like doctors. "Why are they here, Mark?"

"I just want them to check the baby and its heart rate just to make sure everything is still going the way we want it to."

"Grrrrrrrrrrrrrrr mmmmmmmmm. Ok, shit, this hurts so much, they are so close now, and why are they so close?"

He tells me they are just checking but I am feeling scared. Liam walks over to me to give me a hug and I begin to cry, sobbing in fact. The tears are rolling down my swollen cheeks as Mark squeezes my leg and tells me it's going to be ok but we do need to get Baby out now as its heart rate has dropped slightly, it could be a number of reasons but one significant one is maybe the cord is compressed." I think baby just needs a little helping hand to come into this world" The doctors tell Liam to get into some scrubs as we are going into theatre to have a C-section. Mark looks at me and tells me he is going to be there every step of the way. I think I am going to pass out, I feel weird with everything going slightly dark. I'm struggling to catch a breath and I have stars in my eyes, what's going on?"

Liam tells me to breathe normally and to look at him. I am now being wheeled down the corridor to a cold theatre room. Everything is so bright and doctors are everywhere. Another contraction grabs onto me and I try and breathe through it but to be honest, I am losing the will to keep doing it. Mark tell me they are going to give me a spinal so I need to bend over and stay very still whilst they put a needle into my back. I scrunch my head over whilst silently crying and thinking this isn't how it was supposed to go: it was supposed to be easy like Louise why-can't-it-fly-out-with-a-cap-on. Why am I here? The needle has been done so they lay me down and tell me they are going to catheter me. Mark asks my permission to do so.

I am lying there looking up at these huge round lights that are shining brightly down on my stomach. They have put up a sheet just in front of my chest so I can only see from side to side. I have a anaesthetist by my head telling me to stay calm, he will look after me. I can feel someone spraying me with something cold.

"Can you feel that, Sophie?"

"Erm yes."

"Is it cold or just a sensation of spray?"

"It's definitely cold, why?"

"We need to make sure the spinal has worked before we get Baby out. I will leave you a couple of more minutes."

I hear Mark tell one of the others that the catheter has been done then this woman sprays me again. "How's that, is it cold or just a sensation?"

"I think it's ok."

"Great, let's begin then . . ." Liam is by my head telling me how brave I am being. I can feel my palms are sweaty so I don't respond to him as I can feel tears begin to fall again. I can tell you all now I do NOT feel brave, this is the most scared I have ever been as I see Mark out of the corner of my eye watching intently at what the surgeons are doing.

The surgeons are talking to each other in a language only medical ears would understand. Liam is stroking my hair trying to talk to me. I'm not sure what he's saying as I'm not listening, I'm trying to go to my happy place. I shut my eyes and try to pretend that this isn't happening right now, I am in fact sitting in my garden basking in the sunshine enjoying a cocktail with one of those small umbrellas in the top of the glass. All of a sudden I can feel a weird sensation in my stomach like tugging and rummaging around, looking for something. My body is starting to tense up again and I start to sweat and panic. Mark comes to my head and tells me everything is ok, he strokes my cheek and looks at me with sympathetic eyes as tears are still falling from my eyes. I look straight up at the lights that are shining bright and notice small splatters over the shine. The red is vivid . . . shit, that's my blood! Why is it on the lights? What are they doing? Why is my blood up there? Surely it should be inside of me? Breathe Soph, breathe, it's ok. Everyone seems calm so it can't be that bad. Again the more sane side of me comes through. I begin to look around the room at the people I have with me: ok so I have Mark the calm one, I have Liam the worried one then see the other guy next to my head fiddling with the heart monitor checking I'm ok. He looks at me with kind eyes as they're the only things I can see as he is wearing a mask. He has an accent which I can't make out, he might be South African. Across the other side, I can see a petite nurse running around making sure the surgeons have everything they need, then I have two surgeons either side of my stomach, both women chatting about things I don't understand. Mark is still at my side, telling me the baby is about to be born and does Liam want to see the baby come out of my stomach? He looks weird, like part of him is scared and the other part of him is thinking he doesn't want to look like a wimp if he says no so he says yes. Liam kisses my forehead and tells me it's nearly over. Mark leads the way with Liam following closely behind, closer than I have ever seen him be with someone. It looks like he wants to hold his hand! He's almost hiding behind Mark's shoulder like a child would if it's something they want to see but also don't want to either. Actually he looks adorable, almost vulnerable and a side I have never seen before. I know he is going to make the best daddy, I feel so very lucky. My eyes are fixed on Liam and Mark who are both looking at my stomach. I feel a pull from my stomach and more dragging like my stomach is a washing machine and they are pulling all the clothes out after the final spin. Mark is beaming with what looks like tears in his eyes and Liam is looking pale – I'm thinking he's getting smaller as I hear a thud and Mark disappears out of my view. All I can hear is Mark saying Liam's name loudly then suddenly I hear a cry a baby's cry! I look straight up and I catch a glimpse of what I think is our baby; I'm not sure because it's a blur but it's definitely a baby's cry. Mark stands up and puts Liam on a chair, passes him some water. He leaves Liam and rushes over to the surgeon to do something I don't know as I can't see but the baby's crying has stopped. The surgeons look over to me to say congratulations.

"What is it?"

"It's a beautiful baby boy!"

"Really? A boy! Has he got hair?" Mark is suddenly here holding our baby. "Do you want Baby on your chest whilst the ladies stitch you up?"

"Erm, ok I'm a bit scared though, what if I drop him?"

"I'll be here, you won't drop him, I'm just going to sit Liam next to you."

Wow, I have a baby, look at him! He's huge, he has two eyes, one nose, a mouth, two ears, not much hair - that's ok that will grow - I can't see his hands but hope they have counted his fingers and toes. Liam's next to me. "Look at him, Liam, he's just perfect."

"You're perfect Soph, you're so brave and the love that you have already is radiating off you, it's incredible! This little dude is very lucky to have such a perfect mummy."

"Don't forget Daddy too. I saw a very vulnerable side of you in this room, you should show that a little more."

"Feel a bit of a penis if I'm honest, I passed out."

"And that made me fall deeper in love with you." Mark pops his head over mine, "Can I please borrow little bubba to weigh him?" He takes our baby out of my eyesight to weigh him and immediately feel nervous as I can't see where he's gone. I've only held him for five minutes and already he is the most precious thing, I feel such protection for him already. Wow, these feelings are strong, I wonder if it's some sort of hormone that gets released after the baby is born? I dunno but it's weird.

CHAPTER SIXTEEN

FIRST NIGHT

I am now in a side room with a window, it's late and I have been given morphine to help with the pain and to help me sleep. Baby is in a cot next to me, sleeping peacefully. He looks cleaner now that Mark has given him a little wipe down. I can't quite believe I'm a mummy . . . wow, he's going to need me for everything now, that's a huge thought. I am not going to think about that too much, it may freak me out; I'll just stare at him and try to shut my eyes, maybe just hold the side of the cot. Liam is sitting in the chair next to me telling me to sleep. One of the on duty midwives pops her head round the corner of the door to check we are ok. She looks at Liam and says if he wants to go home for a little bit of sleep then he can and that I am in safe hands. "Yeah, go home Liam, I'll be ok, come back in the morning. Could you bring me some supplies like a dressing gown please and slippers?"

"Of course darling. Ok I'll be back first thing in the morning." Liam gives me a gentle kiss, looks in the cot at our baby and leaves.

I can hear a faint weird noise in the distance, I think it's crying - it is crying! Wake up Soph, wake up! I must have fallen asleep, that's my baby crying. I try to sit up but I can't; nothing works. My stomach feels sore, my muscles won't work, my legs feel heavy . . . I try again but it's no good, my mind wants to but my body says no way. I reach for the buzzer when a nurse walks in, "Are you ok sweetheart?"

"Erm, no, I can't sit up, I can't reach my baby, why can't I move?"

"You have just had major surgery darling, they have cut through muscles and they need to heal to work. You need to take things slowly and use your upper body strength to push yourself up." Oh great, I am crying again. "Don't cry sweetheart, I'll help you, that's what I'm here for. Your body has been put through a huge amount of stress, you're exhausted! Then on top of that, you have a new baby to deal with, let me take baby out to the office with me. Are you planning on breastfeeding?"

"Erm, I don't know, I don't really like the idea of it, is that awful?"

"Absolutely NOT darling, it's whatever feels right for you and if you wake up tomorrow and think that you want to give it a go then that's also ok. I am going to give baby a bottle for you as I really feel you need to sleep. My mum always said soldiers go to work healing you when you sleep so let those soldiers go to work ok?"

"That's very kind of you, thank you so much"

"No problem darling, just before you do sleep would you like a little more pain relief?"

"Yes please, it is pinching."

"I'll just ring the bell for someone to grab some whilst I take great pleasure in cuddling your special one."

Drugged up ready to sleep - weird feeling morphine, it's like you're on a floaty cloud. It has made me feel very sleepy but nice sleepy, the sleepy feeling you get on the sofa at home. There is no other feeling like it.

MONDAY 11TH March 2019

Awake early at six o'clock, I am in pain but Baby is back next to me asleep. Still I try to move again as I am uncomfortable. OMG IT'S SO HARD TO MOVE! I feel as if I'm paralysed. I try to move my legs – ok, there is movement there. I dig my heels in the bed and then with my arms I try to push myself up to the back of the bed. Yep, I move three inches but it's a start. Now rest for a minute then let's try again . . . 1 2 3 push, breathe, 1 2 3 push, breathe. That will do, I'm sort of sitting up. Looking out of the window it looks like it's going to be a nice day. I hear movement in the room and look at Baby. Hmmm, what to call you, little one? What do you look like? Do you look like a Jake? Nope. How about a Jackson? Nope. Carter? Nope. Theodore? No way, that reminds me of chipmunks. Zachary? Hmmmmm that might be it: Zachary. . . little baby Zachary. I mean obviously I am going to have to consult with Daddy about your name but how do you feel about that name? Mummy likes it.

The door creeps open and it's Mark with a huge bunch of flowers, he's in his uniform. "Hey darling, how you feeling?"

"Like I've been run over then reversed back over then chucked in a bush!"

"At least you still have your sense of humour, these are for you."

"Oh really, they are just beautiful, you must spend a fortune if you buy all your patients flowers."

"Well, who's to say I buy all of my patients flowers?" Mark winks at me and heads over to look at Zachary– ooops, shouldn't get attached to the name and for Christ sake don't say it loud.

"He is perfect, well done you, you certainly didn't have an easy time."

"Is he ok? I mean because he's early, does he need a lamp or something?"

"No, no, he's a perfect healthy baby weighing in at 6 pounds 7, some full term babies don't even weigh in that big. Can you imagine if you did go full term? Little chunky monkey he would have been."

Mark puts the flowers on the table and helps me sit up slightly more and I wince at the pain, "Let me check your stats see if we can give you something for the pain."

"Are you on shift today?"

"Yes, I don't start until 7.30 though, I wanted to get here early to see you for a little while before babies start flying out all over the place. I'm just going to go get you drugs"

"Thanks Mark."

Mark comes back with the good stuff, am I sounding like a drug addict? Isn't morphine heroin? Or from the same plant? I'm sure I read somewhere it comes from a flower? Mark lifts up Zachary and gives him to me . . . oh crap, I've done it again, called him Zachary. Well, looks like that may be his name; you may witness our first mum and dad fight if Liam doesn't like it. Mark has also brought tea and biscuits, he sits in the chair next to me sipping his tea. "Anyway how are you? I think I remember you telling me you're single now, is that still true?"

"Oh yes, that is still true, she has moved on pretty quickly with her muscly, manly man."

"If you don't mind me saying, she sounds like a right bitch, one you're better off without."

"Yeah I know, it's just hard especially with this job, everyone thinks you're gay. I think you're the only one that just took me for who I am."

"Hmmmmm, out of interest though, why did you get into this job, did you just want to look at fanny all day?" Mark nearly spits out his tea, "What! Erm, no way, do you know what sort of car crash they look like after childbirth?"

"Bloody hell, how can I forget Louise's birth? I know exactly what it looks like? Then why?"

"When I was younger, my mum became pregnant by a bloke who of course left her before the baby was born. I was around eleven or twelve when one night I was woken by a sound which was coming from the bathroom: a grunting, deep, howling noise. I got up, called for Mum, went in her room and she wasn't there. I called again then saw her foot out of the bathroom door, she was on all fours on the floor. I panicked, kept asking her what was wrong until I realised what it was. I ran to get the house phone to call 999 but as the operator picked up I could see things had changed even in that short time just running to get the phone. The operator told me to stay calm and she talked me through what to do as it was obvious my mum wasn't getting to the hospital in time to deliver my sister. So I delivered her on the bathroom floor! I was just amazed at the human body and the strength women have to be able to push a baby out - it blew my mind to see afterwards, the happiness it brought, the joy on my mums face, I will never forget that. It was all I really wanted to do when I left college. My mum is a beautiful soul but chose bad decisions in her life. I tried the manly jobs of bricklaying and labouring but never really loved it, then one day I was drunk and applied to a university to become a midwife and the rest is history."

"Wow Mark, that is inspiring!" He laughs.

Zachary started to make little sounds, not a cry, just a little whine. I think he may need his nappy changed but how am I going to do this when I can't even sit up properly? Mark is up and on it, he takes Zachary and puts him next to me in his cot asking for my consent to change him. He unwraps him as he was all snug like a fajita when he begins to cry and sticks his arms straight out to the sides, resembling a chicken. His legs are so skinny, his fingers are long and bony and his lips are quivering as he cries. His cry isn't bad, I mean you know he's here but it's not too loud. I must be one of the lucky ones as his volume is low. Mark takes his nappy off. Whoa, hold up! What's the matter with his poo? Why is it black, it looks like tar, is he ok?"

"Yes he's fine, that's normal for the first few poos, it's called meconium and it's made up of cells and substances that line the digestive tract during pregnancy."

"Ok, understood none of that but as long as he's ok, yeah?"

"Yeah, it's normal." Zachary is all fajita-wrapped up again and is happy, calm and sleepy. Mark leaves him in his cot and tells me he better go and get ready for handover. As he leaves the room, he looks back at me and sticks his tongue out playfully at me . . . weirdo!

8.30am: Liam arrives with someone following behind, it's Paul holding a blue balloon and looking sheepish. Looking only at the cot I can see he is emotional and he finally looks at me to tell me he's beautiful. Liam is sitting on the edge of the bed also looking sheepish. "You two ok? You're both looking weird, why? What's happened?"

"Nothing."

"You both look sheepish."

"It's probably because we have slightly sore heads this morning as when I got home last night Paul got out the whisky to wet Baby's head."

"WHISKY? You don't even like whisky!"

"I know." Ah, it all makes sense now. Paul has his head over the cot just staring at him. "Don't breathe too close to him please, I don't want your stale whisky breath over my baby."

"We only had a couple Soph, it's just we are not used to drinking it and we were tired and it was late so after a couple, we passed out anyway."

"Still don't want Zachary breathing in any stale breath, thank you."

"Excuse me, ZACHARY?"

"Erm yes, do you like that name?"

"I am not sure, should this not have been a joint decision?"

"Well yeah of course and it was going to be but I woke up early in pain and just was looking at him and I think he looks like a Zachary, don't you?"

"I don't know, he's a baby, he would look like a Slim Shady if you kept calling him that!"

"Can I just interrupt here, Liam and Soph, I personally think Zachary is perfect."

"Do you really Paul?"

"Yeah I do, it's a strong solid name, it will get shortened to ZAC and that sounds cool too." I look at Liam with puppy eyes and he gives in and just lets me have my way and so he should! I have basically been sawn in half and put back together again!

CHAPTER SEVENTEEN

GOING HOME

Wednesday 13th March 2019

This is my third day in hospital now, I am still in pain but yesterday I did manage to walk around and have my catheter out so today. They have told me if I can wee in a cardboard jug and fill it up to the line I can go home. If I'm honest I'm a little scared of going home: I will then be really on my own. At least here I have support. Mark has been in every day, I am going to miss our little chats. I feel I have gained a friend but I am sure he has enough friends, this is his job and he can't stay friends with every pregnant lady he deals with. A weird thing happened this morning: I was sitting there having a cup of tea when Zachary started to cry and before I could even put my tea down, my boobs just started leaking. It was honestly like I was in a wet t-shirt competition, it was the strangest thing. So I know now why you need those massive breast pads: I was soaked. So not only do you need pads for your leaking boobs but you also need a really thick sanitary towel and to top it off, if you have had a C-section you have a huge dressing over your tummy. All of which makes me feel sick every time I look at it. I just cannot understand these women thinking it's easier to have a section than to push, you know the ones to posh to push? Well ladies, let me tell you I feel as if I have been sawn in half. I can't stand up straight, you can't just sit up when you want to sit up, you have to sleep on your back, and you're not allowed to even lift a kettle let alone your own baby. Of course, you have to lift your baby up but when I do I need a pillow on my tummy to protect it, I haven't had a poo yet which I am dreading if I'm honest as just going for a wee, the pressure in your tummy is enough let alone straining for a backed-up poo!

I have a window in my room which looks over the car park to maternity ward and I can see Mum and Dad walking over with the biggest cuddly bear I have ever seen.

"Hello, beautiful baby girl."

"Hey dad."

"Oh my just look at him, he has my looks, I can see this already, he's going to be a handsome young lad!"

Smother just raises her eyebrows at his comment, I thought she may come back with a quick remark but she's managing to hold it in. I can see its killing her to keep her mouth shut but she does. It is like having two children in the room silently fighting over who's being more affectionate to Zachary. They ask me where Liam is.

"He's at home at the moment getting things sorted as I am hoping to go home if I can fill this jug up with pee."

"Bloody hell, that's a lot of pee, you better start drinking darling. Oh by the way, all the girls and clients send their love, we miss you already and there are gifts piling up in the salon for you."

My phone vibrates, it's Amy, Paul's ex. It's a real shame they split up she is nice. I let the phone ring off as I didn't want to be rude with my parents being here, but it vibrates again, this time with a message from her saying congratulations on the birth of our baby and that she needs to talk to me. Weird but I'll chat with her later.

Whilst Mum and Dad are here I might just try a little walk down the corridor and back again to see if I can stand up a little straighter than a 90 year-old hunched over. Every step is a struggle. I feel so heavy and my stomach is so swollen I still look pregnant - not 4 month pregnant, more like 9 month preggers. Walking hunched-like and slower than a snail, I pass rooms with the dreaded noise of birth: yuck, yuck, yuck! Hum your go-to-happy song Soph. Mark has come to find me to ask me if I have filled up the jug yet. "Are you kidding me? Have you seen how big that thing is? I'm never getting out of here!"

"Come on Soph, positive thinking and sips of drink then you'll be surprised. You're walking much better today!"

"Hmmmmm, I don't feel it."

"You seem down, what's up?"

"Not sure, worrying about going home and coping and I am going to miss your face I have got used to you being around."

"You'll be fine at home, you're a natural and you're not alone. Liam will be a great support to you and I suppose I took it for granted that you have just naturally become a friend. I didn't even take into account that I wouldn't see you again."

"Really?"

"Yeah, really."

"If that's ok with you both to still be in your lives."

"Of course!"

"Great, now go and drink some water let's get you out of this joint." Walking back to the room I felt a bit happier.

CHAPTER SEVENTEEN

HOME AT LAST

Still Wednesday . . .

We are home: yayayayayayay!!! I cannot describe the feeling I got when walking through that door but one feeling I definitely had was how lucky I am to be alive as the journey from the hospital to home was almost like being in the game of Grand Theft Auto. I think the whole moron population came out just for my return home. Liam drove way too fast, even if he was only doing 20mph as every bump on the road felt like my stitches were going to pop open and having a seat belt on was painful too. Every pedestrian wanted to cross at every zebra crossing going and also, just to let you know, indicators on cars are there for a reason so bloody use them douchebags! Do they not know I have the most precious thing ever in my life in the car with me? I have only been a mum for five minutes and already I can see that the world is a dangerous place. I have made a decision whilst on the journey home: I am becoming a recluse. Nothing can hurt Zachary if I don't go out . . . I catch a glimpse of the one thing that could hurt him: Pyscho Cat!

"LIAM!"

"Yeah."

"Psycho Cat has got to go."

"What? Why?"

"It's going to smother Zachary in his sleep."

"No its not!"

"Yes it is, I know they like the breath of a new born human so they sit on their face and then it kills them."

"Soph, you're being dramatic."

"Excuse me, DRAMATIC? Well, I do apologise for wanting our baby to grow into an adult."

"Oh, come on Soph."

"Nope, it's fine! Any man knows the word 'fine' does not mean fine so I'll just leave it there for now. As I look around the house I see Paul and Liam have been busy with all the little jobs that have needed doing for the last year. The house is spotless and Zachary's room is just amazing, the soft furnishings are perfect. I wonder whose help they had with picking those. There is a dinner in the slow cooker which smells divine AND a cup of tea has just appeared . . . what more can a girl want? Well, apart from stomach muscles that work and a poo.

The afternoon has been exhausting with family members thinking it's just ok to turn up. I have only been home two hours when the mayhem begins: firstly, my bro and his family, then the in-laws, then Smother pops in even though I saw her earlier, then Louise although she's on her own and you know what, she was the only one I didn't have to tell to wash her hands before holding Zac! Liam thinks I'm CRAZY asking people to wash their hands before a hold but I don't want people's germy hands touching my baby and for Christ sake don't kiss him, don't put your hands anywhere near his mouth, thank you very much. Do you think I'm crazy? So be it if you do, I don't give a rat's arse.

Its 8pm and I'm in pain so I just give Liam the bottle to feed Zachary and think I am going to head off to bed to try and get in a couple of hours before he needs feeding again.

1am and I'm woken by what sounds like a pug sleeping, almost a grunting snuffling noise. I look to my left at the crib and it's Zachary making a noise that's new: no cry, just looking uncomfortable, lifting his little legs up to his tummy. I take my time to sit up . . . I mean, let's be honest here, I can't be quick about anything. I'm going to time myself next time to see how long it takes me to sit up as it's almost like doing an upper body work out every time. Ok, I am now up, oh and so is Paul who is standing in the hallway whispering to me to see if I want any help. As I slowly stand up, I ask him if he could pick Zachary up and take him into his nursery. Paul looks happy to help, he looks so fresh and alive for 1am. He grabs Zac and heads off to the nursery room whilst I take one step at a time to go down stairs, again pondering why we didn't buy a bungalow. Every step is a goal. It's amazing what your stomach muscles are attached to because even lifting my legs to go down the stairs I can feel my tummy pinching and pulling with every step . . . IT'S SO CRAP!

Why does it take so long for a bottle to cool down? The grunting has gone into full-blown crying now and I can hear Paul upstairs trying to calm him down. I cannot however hear Liam . . . bloody typical, sleeping through his own baby crying. As I head SLOWLY back upstairs, I don't hear crying anymore but maybe I have gone deaf as Zachary has been screaming the house down for the last ten minutes! Just maybe my ear drums have thought, stuff this for a laugh, you're on your own! Nope, scrap that, I can hear Psycho coughing up a hair ball; crisis averted, I still have working ears.

In the nursery, Paul is sitting on the rocking chair gently rocking Zachary whilst singing him a song. Zachary looks so content, he isn't asleep but he is happy looking up at Paul who is smiling at me. I hand him the bottle, "Well done, he is obviously happy with you so if you want to, you can feed him."

"Really?"

"Yes really"

"But I have never fed a baby before!"

"Now's the time to learn, I'll stay with you."

I get back into bed about 2 o'clock trying to get comfy. I have a row of pillows dividing the bed as I fear Liam rolling onto my tummy but he is still sound asleep. Woken up at 5am by Zachary wanting food again . . .

Thursday 14th March 2019

8am rolls round and Paul pops his head into the lounge to say bye as he's off to work. Liam is still in bed ASLEEP! I am going to lose my shit soon as I am the one who has had a bloody C-section and am still managing to feed our baby at night but not only that, his best mate on Zac's first night home got up in the middle of the night and calmed him.

10am and Liam finally gets up; I am so fuming I can't even look at him, he knows I am angry but doesn't know why - he knows. He makes me a tea to see if that calms me and guess what, IT DOESN'T but I am not going to tell him as I feel my hormones are all over the place. Instead, I'll check back with myself later.

My phone rings, its Amy again.

"Hey Soph, how are you feeling? Congratulations on the baby."

"I am feeling like I have been run over by a bus!"

"I have a present for you but I didn't want to make things awkward by popping it round as I know that Paul is living with you at the moment."

"Don't be silly Amy, it won't be awkward. We are all grown-ups plus its nothing to do with us, it's your business and if Paul feels awkward whilst you're here then he can go out. You never know, it may give you guys a chance to talk."

"I think talking is over."

"Well you never know, but certainly pop over. Just text me before you do so I can at least try and get dressed."

"Of course, I'll give you lots of notice before I do but it is so lovely to speak to you, I have been putting it off calling you."

"You silly mare, never feel like that!"

"Anyway, I'll catch up very soon Soph, congrats again."

"Thank you, see you soon, bye."

Its 4pm and I am still not dressed, not washed, teeth not done, and dry shampoo saving me for another day, the only thing I have accomplished today was a POO! All hail the Poo Lord! It was intense with many fears washing over me whilst sitting on the toilet: 1.. will my stitches come undone and make my insides just fall out? 2.. will my piles get worse so that I have grapes hanging out of my backside forever? 3.. I have had so many stool softeners to help with this situation so what if I have taken too many and once it begins it never stops and overflows the toilet? 4.. will I pass out afterwards, leaving Liam having to scoop me and my dirty butt off the floor? Reality check: it wasn't pleasant but none of the above happened so happy days.

Paul is home, I mention Amy calling and he goes a very pale shade of magnolia. "That's nice, did she have much to say?"

"No, only congratulations and she is going to pop over soon."

"When?"

"I dunno, not today."

"Oh ok, she say anything else?"

"Nope"

"Ah ok cool. He so still loves her, I can tell the Cilla Black in me may need to work her magic once more.

CHAPTER EIGHTEEN

EMOTIONS

WEDNESDAY 27TH March 2019

It's been a whole two weeks since bringing Zachary home and I am starting to feel a little better. I still lay on my side and still very slow and swollen but laughing and sneezing has got slightly easier. Mark and Smother have been amazing with Mark cheering me up with his gossip and funny memes and Smother here ready and waiting to help with cleaning, cooking and just being a beautiful Nanny that she is. Mark has popped round to see if I fancied a gentle walk down the road. How far are we going? Do I need everything for Zac?"

"No, we are only going up and down the road to get your muscles slowly working again."

"Ok shall I leave Zachary here with Liam?"

"If you want to, we will only be ten minutes."

"Ok I can cope with that."

I am outside and wow, it's so bright and feels strange being out and having no baby. Pavements are uneven and I am worried about tripping up. Mark tells me to take his arm for support, it's so strong. I always forget how tall he is, I almost feel like a child next to him. He begins to tell me about the dates he has been on, describing one girl as stunning but had nothing else about her; I instantly disliked her although not sure why, just a feeling I had. Walking and talking was really nice, I felt slightly more human I must say, although I am shattered, even just that short walk really has taken it out of me.

Back home, quick tea and Mark says his goodbyes. I go to the sofa with Liam to chill out. "Nice walk?"

"Yeah, really lovely thanks, was Zachary ok whilst I was gone?"

"Yes he slept the whole 15 minutes that you were away."

"Don't be funny, it's a huge thing leaving him."

"I'm joking Soph, don't take it to heart. How's Mark's boyfriend anyway, are they back together? I know they had a fight when you were in labour."

Oh balls, Liam doesn't know he's not gay. "Erm, boyfriend? Don't you mean girlfriend?"

"What?"

"He isn't gay, what gave you that idea?"

"Eh? Everything?"

"Like what, just because he's a midwife? That is very small minded of you, Liam."

"No Soph, even you thought he was gay."

"When?"

"ALWAYS!"

"Nope, I wouldn't be that small minded to judge."

"Oh shut up Soph, don't give me that bullshit, so you're telling me this whole time he hasn't been gay?"

"Yep that's what I'm telling you."

"BLOODY HELL so why is he still hanging around?"

"Because he is my friend!"

"Hmmm I am not so sure about that, I think he fancies you."

"Liam, five minutes ago you were fine with our relationship and thought he fancied you! Now the tables have turned and the reality is that he's not gay, you think he fancies me and that's the only reason why we are friends?"

"Bluntly, yes."

"I have nothing to respond to that, only that I have just had your baby, we are happily married and I might be a person that people want to befriend."

"Yep all of that, let's leave it there, Soph."

"Yep, let's leave it there."

Tears. Where do they come from? One minute I am absolutely fine and the next I am a blubbering mess, I just don't get it. Everything hits you at once: joy, anxiety, sheer panic, sadness then pure fear. Maybe I have a hormone imbalance or maybe I am one of those people that snaps and ends up doing something terrible. OH CRAP I definitely don't want that, I better call someone who knows about this stuff. I end up texting Louise who knows about this as she's had two. I mean, I could call Smother but she would be marching me down to A&E telling the doctors I have a brain tumour.

Hey Lou, how ya doing? Quick question, when you had your babies did you feel as if you were going slightly mental with all the different emotions and hormones, when does this stop?

Her reply comes quickly.

Hey Babes, what do you mean stop???? This is your life now, get used to it. Your emotions will be heightened forever more, welcome to the club, why do you think we drink! Hope you're coping ok, I'll be over at some point next week with Dan and the kids, always here for you. Big hugs xxxx

Why did I ask her anyway? I am sure I read somewhere your hormones just need to settle, it's been a traumatic time for everyone involved. What is that noise that sounds like someone is gagging? I walk upstairs to find Liam in the nursery standing over Zachary attempting to change his nappy with has a scarf wrapped around his mouth and nose . . . Liam?"

"Bit busy at the mo Soph, omg, this is just wrong! Why does it smell so bad and is the colour of chicken tikka masala? I'm not sure I can carry on Soph, I need your help!"

I ignore him as I am too busy laughing. I have tears streaming down my cheeks, finding it hard to breathe. My stomach is hurting, I have to walk out of the room. I lean against my bed trying to get the image out of my head but I just keep laughing. Liam walks in. "Thanks for your help, I could have vomited all over our son!"

"No you wouldn't have, the scarf would have caught most of it."

"Such a supporting wife I have!"

"You have to get used to it Liam, they are only going to get worse, Babe."

"Worse than that - you can't get worse than that! It was like acid burning my eyeballs and nose hair, what could possibly be worse?"

"Oh stop Liam, my stomach hurts enough. I don't want to laugh anymore."

Paul is home and he is abnormally quiet, I try to talk to him but he doesn't want to talk. I tell Liam to take him out for a drink to see if he's ok. 11pm rolls round and when they walk in, I am standing in the kitchen with the door slightly closed. They are giggling and whispering to each other as they walk into the kitchen not expecting me to be there. I startle them and Liam looks stunned as this is the latest I have been up in two weeks. "Sorry, are we too loud?"

"No its ok, I was just going to bed with a feed for Zac." Paul has gone sheepish again and scuttles off to bed as I ask if he's ok. "Yeah, he's ok, just tired I think, anyway I'll come up with you."

CHAPTER NINETEEN

GUT

Monday 1st April

The days go past so quickly and the time has come for Liam to go back to work. I am fearing this but also looking forward to it as I feel we are both getting on each other's nerves. He has been different the last two days, very distant. Even with Paul, he hasn't been right; they are trying to act like mates but I can feel something is up so I think he needs to go back to work to get whatever is in his system out. First thing I notice is how tranquil it is! The only thing I have to worry about now on my own is Psycho Cat trying to smother the baby as when there were two of us around, Zachary has never been left in a room on his own for longer than 5 minutes but I can't carry on like that. I must start to put him in his crib to sleep otherwise I'll have a cling-on child forever. I think I will put something in front of the cat flap whilst on my own, I mean, it's a nice day and Psycho will enjoy the sunshine. My phone buzzes, it's Amy asking to pop over so I say of course. She says she will bring cake . . . yummy, you can't go wrong with cake. Two hours pass and Amy arrives looking beautiful, she has certainly made an effort; skinny jeans, tight top, I think she has had her teeth whitened, her hair is a pale blonde, cut into a short sharp bob which is fabulous. She walks in, coos over Zachary for a while then we tuck into cake and drink tea as tells me that she has been struggling with the breakup between her and Paul. I ask why they actually broke up and she says she doesn't know, he just walked in one night and said he couldn't do it anymore and needed space to get his head together. She thinks there is someone else and asks me if there is but I can only tell her what I know and that's nothing. I tell her I don't think there is anyone as he rarely goes out and he is very sweet and helpful with Zac. I am not sure she believes me so I suggest she stays for dinner.

"I don't think so, I think that would be awkward."

"No, it won't and if he doesn't like it, he can go out."

"I'm not sure."

"Oh come on Amy, are you telling me you dress up like this every day?"

"Yeah, why?"

"Oh nothing, you look fab, that's all, let's show him what's he's missing!"

"Oh ok."

"Fabulous, I'll go and start prepping whilst you have a cuddle." She dresses like that every day, SHUT UP, DOES SHE HELL.

5.30 comes around and Liam walks in first then followed swiftly by Paul. Amy is in the lounge and I'm in the kitchen. They are both like a couple of kids as they head straight to the fridge, starving as usual. "When's dinner?"

"About half an hour."

"Paul, I have something to tell you, it's Amy."

"Right, what about Amy?"

"She's in the lounge."

"WHAT?"

"Yeah, don't freak out, she's staying for dinner."

"What? When?"

"Tonight."

"Oh Soph, really!" Liam's look tells me I have crossed a line. Oops, I feel a bit bad now, what shall I do? Paul walks into the lounge and shuts the door behind him as Liam is pacing up and down in the kitchen looking at me with evil eyes, "Don't look at me like that, please!"

"You had no right Soph, no right at all!"

"I'm sorry but she was sad, she doesn't know why they split up. Apparently, Paul just walked out, no reason whatsoever."

"He has his reasons. Just because he doesn't tell the world, he has reasons!"

"Well, she thinks he has someone else." Liam stops talking and walks out. Now what do I do? I think I have made a pig's ear of this situation. Ok, think Soph . . . I know, I'll just carry on with dinner as planned. If no one is at the table to eat it I'll treat it as an eating trial and demolish the lot myself, I need to keep my strength up anyway.

Dinner was interesting. They all sat round the table with me filling everyone's glasses up with wine, trying to soften the mood which, let me tell you, didn't work. Stuff this, I am having a glass of wine; I'm not breastfeeding so I can. Woah, that is strong wine! I look at the bottle to see what strength it is and oh, it's normal strength yet just one glass and I feel pissed. I look around the table at the sad faces looking back at me; this is some dull dinner! Amy just keeps looking at Paul - you know the look when you were at school and you fancied someone and couldn't help but keep looking at them but that person doesn't even know you exist? Sad times and I had many of those. You have Paul, just head down, eating as fast as he can to obviously get away from this situation. Then there is Liam trying to make small chat with Paul and also giving me the evils so all in all great dinner, I say.

Amy has left the building and I'm taking the plates out to the kitchen where Paul is washing up. I take a moment to apologise to him which he accepts. This evening, we all sit down to a film but Liam's phone keeps going off with text messages, I ask him who they are from and he says it's a bloke from work moaning about a job they have been doing. I have a gut feeling he is lying to me but I won't let that thought consume me; I know I could just be being silly as Amy's worries may have rubbed off onto me. I think of something else and actually . . . what a silly cow I am! He doesn't go anywhere, his first day back to work was today and we have just had a baby! Gosh, I'm sounding deluded, just like him earlier with the whole Mark thing.

Another night, another sound-beating from baby Zac. His cries are not so subtle anymore, even Shrek is stirring when he yells. I mean, he sort of grunts at me then goes back to sleep but the way Zachary looks up at me at 2am is adorable. He looks up at me in the day too but at night it seems special, our time: silent apart from the deafening screams before his milk. Once that bottle is in his mouth however, and his tiny hands are squeezing my fingers and his big eyes are looking up at me, I know there's something special in that bond. I know whatever happens in life, he will always need his mummy and I will always need my son.

CHAPTER TWENTY

BAD DAYS

SATURDAY 15TH JUNE 2019

Zac is three months old now and let me tell you, these last few weeks have been testing. I have not slept solidly since he was born, I'm constantly tired and I have my hair in a mum bun every day because to be honest, just having a wash is pushing it, let alone doing your bloody hair and make-up - what's make-up ? I think if I had to put some on now, I would look like Crusty the Clown as I don't remember what to do with make-up anymore. Zachary is amazing though, he is mostly happy unless hungry which actually is a lot of the time so you could say he is 50/50 but still amazing. Paul is still living here, I think as a permanent fixture now. I really don't mind as some nights he gets up with me when Zachary is moaning and brings me up a tea. We sit and chat and giggle about silly stuff, mostly about Liam whilst he sleeps. The other night we even came downstairs and had cake which was bloody awesome!

Louise is my counsellor in life, I am always on the phone to her. In fact, the other day I face-timed her whilst sitting on the loo because outside of the bathroom I could hear Zachary crying when Liam was giving him his milk but obviously not doing it right. I can tell when Zac is happy or not but Liam was getting stressed, asking our son why he doesn't like him which was pissing me off. I knew if I went out there it would be game over, Liam would have given in and handed me back the baby so I faced-timed Louise to take my mind off it and to ask her was I doing the right thing. Is it that bad that Zachary wants me constantly? Her reply to me was that I stay in that bathroom until that twat of a husband stops being so melodramatic, puts on his big boy pants and deals with being a dad on the tough days. And that I understand that! So I put the phone down and go straight out of the bathroom to save my son from his moaning father.

Smother and Dad are just loving being Grandparents, they have even decorated their spare bedroom for him, asking me when he can stay over the night or for the both of us to have a sleepover a bonding night which would actually be lovely. I could maybe get a few hours' sleep then. That's it, I have decided I am going to phone them right now. 5o'clock rolls round and I tell Liam I am going to stay at my Mum and Dads for the night. He tries to act disappointed but I can tell he's lying. Why, you may ask? Because he has just fist-pumped the air behind my back which I saw from my peripheral vision and Paul laughed so that means it they are clearly going to get very drunk and play loud shit music. Still, I am super-excited about my sleepover with Mum, its only Mum now as Dad has gone on a Golf weekend. Mum is so excited she has rang me seven times asking when I was coming.

I think I have everything I need, it looks as if I am moving out, I have so many bags. Liam kindly helps me to the car – well, I say kindly but I think he just wants me gone - waving me off and blowing kisses into the air as I drive down the road. Driving is definitely a different experience with your baby in the car as before Zachary I would have old-school tunes blaring away but now, NO WAY! Music is a distraction on the road when I have to focus on the terrible drivers that seem to all be in my town. How they ever passed their tests, I don't know but disgraceful driving, some of them.

Pulling up outside Mum and Dad's house and I should have guessed that she is waiting outside for me. She has a smile of the cat that has got the cream and at my car door before you can even say *super-duper-fragalistic*. I have just put my handbrake on and Smother is at my door yanking at the handle to try and open it which of course it doesn't as I have all the doors locked now as soon as I drive anywhere because of exactly this situation: mad people trying to get into your car. I slowly open my door to hear her ask what took me so long.

"Sorry, it's harder than you think leaving the house with a baby . . . but she's too busy telling me how she has so much planned. Oh no, is it too late to turn back now? I was hoping to fall asleep at 8pm and sleep until 7am, looks like Smother has other ideas.

Wow and double wow, this is incredible! Mum has made her lounge into a spa: it's dark with about a hundred candles everywhere - which sorry, I'll be blowing out any minute as fire hazard comes to mind but it looks beautiful - and even a foot spa and two glasses with a bottle of non-alcoholic rose chilling. She knows I can't handle drink at the moment and says she wants me to relax and not throw up whilst I am here. There are sweets, chocolate and the telly is on with any Sky movie ready to rent - it's just perfect! I blow out all the candles and give her the biggest cuddle, my mum will always be my best friend and I am truly lucky in life.

Pjs are on, mum is snuggling Zac, I am having the best time eating chocolate and watching an old favourite, Pretty Woman, on the telly, my feet have gone like prunes as I've had them in this water so long, I've a green face mask on and

I am living my best life right now, super-relaxed and Mum hasn't stopped smiling since I got here.

Its 10pm and Mum gives Zachary a feed before we head to bed. I was smart, having already made up a bottle before I came out so all Mum had to do was shake the little pot of pre-measured milk into his bottle. I knew she would want to feed him and I didn't want to step on her toes and tell her she was doing it wrong so I thought ahead. I climb into bed with Mum and it's like being a child again. She tells me to sleep soundly and that she will get up when Zachary needs feeding; the feeling I have right now is amazing, I am so excited about having at least 6 hours solid sleep. In fact, I'm not sure I can actually sleep now, I'm too excited about it.

What's that noise? Where am I? That's Zachary crying, what time is it? 2am . . . Where's mum? Why is she not feeding him? I am getting up to see if she is ok. "Mum!"

"I'm in the kitchen."

"Are you ok?"

"I can't find his milk."

"It's in the bag."

"I have looked 5 times."

"Ok give me the bag."

"It's not in there Soph."

"It must be, I packed for leaving home for a year!"

"I am telling you now, it's not."

"SHIT, SHIT, SHIT, it's not!"

"I know!"

"What are we going to do Mum?"

"I have some Weetabix we could give him, that with hot milk?"

"You can't do that, he isn't supposed to have real milk until he is a year old!"

"A year? That's bollocks, excuse my French. You were on solids at this age, you loved your food."

"Times change Mum, the guidelines are twelve months, I'm going to have to go home and get some."

"It's 2am Sophie, this is the time the weirdos walk the streets and gangs prey on young women driving alone, you can't possibly go home!"

"Zachary needs feeding Mum, I'm going, just rock him whilst I am gone, I'll only be half an hour."

"Lock your doors!"

"I already do Mum."

"Ok drive safe."

What a useless mother I am, I can't even remember my baby's milk and I knew I was too excited about sleep - look at me now, driving at 2.20am in my dressing gown! If I get stopped by the police, I would lock me up! I don't pull up on the driveway as I don't want the dog to go mental and start barking, so decide to pull up a couple of houses away and try and sneak in. I don't want to wake up the boys. Why is everything so loud at night time? You would think it's my first time opening a door… making so much noise!

Ok I am in, I go straight to the kitchen to grab the milk, quickly tip-toeing through the hall, I see the telly in the lounge is still on. Honestly, they can't even remember to turn the telly off and it's too loud. How can they sleep through that? I'll turn it off on my way back out. In the kitchen, there it is: the magic powder, almost shining like treasure. Actually, thinking about it, why didn't Liam call me to tell me I had forgotten it? Honestly, it's becoming more obvious that the only person you can rely on is yourself. Back to the task in hand, got the milk and I'll just go into the lounge carefully as one of them may be asleep on the sofa. I push the lounge door open slowly, and OH. MY. GOD! I can't believe what I am witnessing – NO! NO! NO! Wake up Soph, it's not real, shit…I think I am going to throw up!

"Paul . . . Liam? What are you doing?

They suddenly stopped kissing each other and quickly turned to me, with a look of fear and shock imprinted onto their faces . . .

THE END

Printed in Great Britain
by Amazon

56277616R00088